Eduardo Gut

The Gaucho Juan Moreira

True Crime in Nineteenth-Century Argentina

EDUARDO GUTIÉRREZ

The Gaucho Juan Moreira

True Crime in Nineteenth-Century Argentina

Translated by
John Charles Chasteen

Edited, with an Introduction, by
William G. Acree, Jr.

Hackett Publishing Company, Inc.
Indianapolis/Cambridge

Copyright © 2014 by Hackett Publishing Company, Inc.

17 16 15 14   1 2 3 4 5 6 7

For further information, please address
    Hackett Publishing Company, Inc.
    P.O. Box 44937
    Indianapolis, Indiana 46244-0937

    www.hackettpublishing.com

Interior and cover design by Elizabeth L. Wilson
Composition by Aptara, Inc.

Cover image: José Podestá dressed in full gaucho garb to perform in a Creole drama, 1890. We see the poncho slung over his shoulder; wide *tirador* around his waist; riding whip in his left hand; *chiripá* covering his legs; and the unmistakable *botas de potro*, with his toes hanging out. *Archivo General de la Nación, Dpto. Doc. Fotográficos*, Argentina.

Map on p. xxxviii by Jennifer A. Moore, GIS Librarian, Washington University in St. Louis

Library of Congress Cataloging-in-Publication Data

Gutiérrez, Eduardo, 1851–1889.
    [Juan Moreira. English]
    The gaucho Juan Moreira : true crime in nineteenth-century
Argentina / Eduardo Gutierrez ; translated by John Charles Chasteen ;
edited, with an introduction, by William G. Acree, Jr.
        pages cm
    Includes bibliographical references.
    ISBN 978-1-62466-136-5 (pbk.) — ISBN 978-1-62466-137-2 (cloth)
    1. Moreira, Juan, 1819–1874—Fiction. 2. Gauchos—Argentina—
Fiction. I. Chasteen, John Charles, 1955– translator. II. Title.
    PQ7797.G79J813 2014
    863'.5—dc23   2014000562

∞

CONTENTS

Translator's Note   vii

Introduction   ix

Suggested Readings   xxxv

Map of Moreira's Movements   xxxviii

The Gaucho Juan Moreira   1

Glossary   117

TRANSLATOR'S NOTE

Juan Moreira is an action story. Many things happen in it, and sometimes they happen repeatedly. While there is great emphasis on Moreira's feelings, those feelings are unchanging. What occurs here occurs in the physical world. The fight scenes are rendered blow by blow, with great visual clarity, as if intended to be filmed. I have labored to be faithful to this magnificent story, above all, by keeping the action as vivid as possible.

That means, first, privileging action over authorial commentary. In true nineteenth-century style, Gutiérrez tells us specifically how to react to the triumphs and tribulations of the man he often calls "our hero," but modern readers soon tire of being told that the scene they are reading is sad or thrilling, especially when the scenes speak so well themselves. Therefore, authorial commentary of that sort has been pruned of its frequent repetitions. Second, the original Spanish version of the story is also slowed by other sorts of repetition linked to the ways in which a *folletín* was written and read. Gutiérrez produced installments of *Juan Moreira* much as student authors tend to produce their own texts: for publication (so to speak) within hours. Sometimes (dare I say it?) he padded his text to reach a desired length, especially, I believe, with redundant descriptions of Moreira's emotional wounds. He also often repeated basic exposition because the readers of today's *folletín* had not necessarily read yesterday's installments. Imagine a television serial that begins episodes with quick reminders of previous events. *The Gaucho Juan Moreira*, in English, has been considerably shortened by the minimization of all these repetitions.

In addition, an English version of a gaucho story sometimes needs to explain (not merely translate) things that have no English equivalents because they are, if not *uniquely* Argentine (or Uruguayan), not far from it. Moreover, gaucho speech, as represented by authors in the "*gauchesque*" tradition, is loaded with local color, proverbs, and dialect—things which translate not at all. Gaucho stories must be adapted, not simply translated, for a modern English-language readership.

For these reasons (and because it is frequently in verse) *gauchesque* literature has rarely been translated.

This is the first appearance of *Juan Moreira* in English. It has been adapted in many ways for a new readership, but it's still exactly the same movie, so to speak, that Eduardo Gutiérrez created, without knowing it, in 1879–1880. And it's a doozy.

INTRODUCTION

A Mythical Gaucho and the Making
of Modern Popular Culture

The gaucho Juan Moreira, with his splendid horse, his fancy garb, and, above all, his fearsome weapons, was an actual man, but he also became a mythic hero. Like U.S. cowboys, Argentine gauchos faced their rivals, one on one, in deadly duels, but they fought with knives instead of six-shooters. Juan Moreira became known as the greatest fighter of them all. His blade of Toledo steel was unstoppable, and his wit, just as sharp. He also showed his style on the dance floor, where few could match his footwork, and with the guitar. His chord progressions and improvisational verses captivated even the most callous hearts. In one bloody encounter after another, he avenged himself on those who had victimized him and driven him to crime, then vanquished a string of gaucho challengers and, all the while, wreaked havoc on the police squads sent to capture him. Nothing could save him, however, from the downward legal, moral, and physical spiral that ended in his death in April 1874. That narrative is what Eduardo Gutiérrez presents in this great classic of Argentine "true crime" writing.

The importance of this true crime story goes far beyond the life of the famous outlaw. Juan Moreira became an icon of Argentine popular culture and has remained one ever since, in print, on stage, and at the movies. In fact, *Juan Moreira* was arguably *the best-selling text of any kind in all* of Latin America prior to the twentieth century. Snobs hated the book and considered its author, Eduardo Gutiérrez, to be a literary hack. Yet even the most ardent critics simply could not ignore the massive reading public that Gutiérrez reached and, moreover, actually helped create. This last point is of enormous importance. Before the radio theater of the 1930s, 1940s, and 1950s (where the story of Moreira also glued listeners to their speakers) and close to a century before *telenovelas* began captivating audiences from the United States down to Argentina, the greatest medium of written storytelling in Latin America were the *folletines*—narratives published serially in the newspaper—and among these *Juan Moreira* was king. Records of print runs of both the newspaper and later book editions of *Moreira* dwarfed other titles from the same years. Readers camped out at the office of the newspaper that published this folletín, avidly awaiting the next installment of *Moreira*. The commercial success of *Moreira*, as well as its movement from the newspaper to the inexpensive book format, from the circus stage to the silver screen, point to the narrative's role in the making of modern popular culture in nineteenth-century Argentina.

What was it about this narrative that captured the attention of Argentines (and Uruguayans, too) so forcefully for so long? What can we learn from it about the bustling, rapidly transforming societies that adored this swashbuckling hero? Let's saddle up, with some necessary background on the author, the cultural milieu in which he worked, and the history of Argentina in the 1800s.

Eduardo Gutiérrez and Argentine Popular Culture

Eduardo Gutiérrez wrote feverishly. From the first publication of *Juan Moreira* in the Buenos Aires newspaper *La Patria Argentina* (November 1879–January 1880) to his untimely death from tuberculosis at the age of thirty-eight in 1889, Gutiérrez penned more than thirty folletines as well as a handful of books. He wrote day and night, becoming one of Argentina's first professional authors, aside from one of its most prolific. Of course, being a folletinista was not exactly a mark of distinction among the exclusive "generation of 1880" in Argentina—the group of politicians and intellectuals who held the reins of state power and who, from their perch in the rapidly growing city of Buenos Aires, were overseeing a program of state building and modernization to its peak. Reflecting on *Juan Moreira* and a handful of Gutiérrez's other recent publications, one of the members of this generation wrote, "There is only one way to understand these vulgar serial novels. They constitute the most unhealthy and pernicious literature that has ever been written in Argentina."[1] Another detractor asserted that *Juan Moreira* and similar narratives were corrupting the most basic notions of morality and instilling in the lower classes a rebellious spirit

---

1. *Anuario bibliográfico de la República Argentina. Año II 1880* (Buenos Aires: Imprenta de M. Biedma, 1881), 287.

against authority. The commentator lamented that Gutiérrez calculated his tales expressly to inflame the "hot tempers, roaming imaginations, and the simple feelings" of "errant rural folk. . . . One could even say that in Gutiérrez's work the pleasures of the novelist become confused with the murderous actions of criminals!"[2] Nobody could say, though, that it wasn't popular.

In fact, Gutiérrez's folletines (and the subsequent spread of the story to the circus, the theater, the opera, the cinema, and a host of other media) laid the foundation of Argentina's modern popular culture industry. Let's turn our attention to this popular culture, where we'll see how *gauchesque* (gaucho-like) literature and its connection to oral traditions over the 1800s heightened the appeal of Gutiérrez's narrative. First, though, what exactly do we mean by popular culture?

There are various definitions of popular culture that point to features of its development over time. First, when the concept of popular culture began to take shape in nineteenth-century Latin America (as well as elsewhere in the world) it often included elements of folklore and referred to behaviors, practices, or social norms of popular or marginalized classes. It embodied folkways and modes of communication that bumped up against more "refined" attitudes and behaviors, and not coincidentally this binary vision of culture split along rural-urban divides. If you get the sense of a high-low dichotomy coming into view, that's no mistake. But in spite of the bad rap popular culture has received throughout history, it is "everyday culture."[3] This is what one Argentine intellectual finally (and reluctantly) acknowledged in a 1913 speech to a group of men sitting stiffly at the University of Buenos Aires: "Eduardo Gutiérrez," he told them with a sigh, "is *still* the daily bread of readers and spectators from the suburbs and the country."[4]

Throughout the 1800s "everyday culture" in Argentina benefitted from ample diffusion through oral, visual, written, and other forms of communication, and these all enjoyed wide reception. The voices of African descendants, indigenous groups, poor city residents, and,

---

2. Martín García Merou, *Libros y autores* (Buenos Aires: Félix Lajouane, 1886), 13–24.

3. William H. Beezley and Linda A. Curcio-Nagy, eds., *Latin American Popular Culture: An Introduction* (Wilmington: SR Books, 2000), xi.

4. Carlos Octavio Bunge, "El derecho en la literatura gauchesca." *Discurso leído ante la Academia de Filosofía y Letras de la Universidad de Buenos Aires* (Buenos Aires: Academia de Filosofía y Letras, 1913).

of course, gauchos, came through in popular verse, song, and dance. Likewise, humor (or vulgarity) and playful or serious references to violence, be these written, improvised in song, or stitched into headbands rural residents commonly wore, were consistent attributes of the expression of everyday culture. The uses of popular culture also tied it to daily work patterns, entertainment and leisure, and ceremonial actions at fairs and festivals. All of these characteristics came together in one of the most distinctive manifestations of Argentine and Uruguayan popular culture: *gauchesque* literature.

The *gauchesque* was a form of writing that developed over the course of the 1800s. *Gauchesque* authors put the gaucho voice into print by incorporating vocabulary, syntax, and modes of speech from country inhabitants, often with charged political goals in mind. The earliest known examples of the *gauchesque* were from anonymous authors in the late 1700s and early 1800s, when a series of plays that enjoyed a decades-long run mocked Iberian residents and pseudo-intellectuals and celebrated rural characters. Mocking one's enemy was definitely one of Bartolomé Hidalgo's favorite rhetorical devices during the decade of the 1810s.

An Uruguayan who had moved to Buenos Aires, Hidalgo became the *gauchesque*'s first major author. He employed the *gauchesque* as a literature of outreach to communicate a nativist, American spirit during the wars of independence. His formulas were simple: short, memorable verses full of humor, stinging wit, and country wisdom as well as dialogues between gauchos that often began with one friend arriving at the ranch of another, unsaddling, and settling down with a bitter *mate* to relate the latest news. These formulas stuck, and subsequent generations of *gauchesque* authors scribbled dialogues and similar verses, occasionally including names of Hidalgo's now easily recognizable characters. During the extended period of civil war that engulfed the Río de la Plata (the area encompassing Argentina and Uruguay) from the 1820s through the 1850s, hundreds of loose-leaves and dozens of newspapers with *gauchesque* verse, edited by "gaucho gazetteers," played a central role in the politicization of popular classes. Envisioning such verses read aloud to a group of men drinking and laughing at a *pulpería* (the local dry goods store that doubled as a watering hole) provides a good example for visualizing this popular culture in action.

As the dust on the battlefields settled, *gauchesque* authors turned their attention from political persuasion to aesthetic goals and humor, though social concerns were never far away (take, for example, the long poem *Fausto* from 1866 that tells of a gaucho's impressions at an opera in Buenos Aires' fancy opera house). In the 1870s another phase of the *gauchesque* began, which lamented transformations the period's great export boom was exacting on traditional ways of life and the changing social place of the gaucho. A clear example is José Hernández's epic poem *The Gaucho Martín Fierro* (1872, along with its sequel *The Return of Martín Fierro*, 1879), which was a hit among both urban and rural readers and listeners. Illiterate peasants memorized verses from readings they heard of *Fierro* (both parts), and pirated re-editions abounded. In fact, Martín Fierro was the *second* most famous gaucho in Argentina (and Uruguay), behind Juan Moreira, until the early 1900s, when official support for identifying a national poem and bard launched Fierro into first place.

Martín Fierro and *Juan Moreira* initiated a thirty-year boom of *gauchesque* prose and poetry beginning in the 1880s, much of which picked up on themes of these earlier works. This was the most fertile moment of a related literary and cultural movement known as *criollismo*. Criollismo derived its significance from Creole (*criollo*), a colonial term denominating Spaniards born in the Americas and their privileged social status. By the second half of the 1800s, however, Creole had been stripped of all references to Spain. Its new meaning was an inversion of the original and defined what and who were "authentically" Argentine or Uruguayan and clearly *not* European. The turn-of-the-century criollismo craze left lasting impressions, one of the most visible being the creation of Creole societies whose members dressed in gaucho attire, held festive gatherings, and paraded on horseback through city centers. And then in 1927 the novel *Don Segundo Sombra* provided a final installment for the *gauchesque* with a gaucho protagonist who seemed to pass almost completely into the realm of myth.

From this quick overview of the *gauchesque*, readers can glean several enduring characteristics. First, the *gauchesque* from its earliest manifestations up through the early twentieth century was politically and socially committed literature. Second, authors of the *gauchesque* were usually not gauchos themselves, but many had spent a great deal of time in frontier settings, absorbing chatter at pulperías and imitating or transcribing things they had heard. The result was a unique combination of oral and print traditions. Lastly, this type of writing attracted *and* created an enormous audience.

A successful print run for a work of conventional "literature" on European models at the end of the 1800s was, for Argentina, in the range of a couple thousand copies in circulation. *Martín Fierro* passed the sixty thousand mark with ease by 1900, while *Juan Moreira* had sold even more—and these numbers do not even account for pirated

One of the Regules Creole Society members in full gaucho regalia. *Sociedad Criolla Elías Regules*, Montevideo, Uruguay.

editions. This is not altogether surprising, though. In the Americas there is something special about a good cowboy story. It speaks to a specific identity often associated with adventure and heroism, frontier life and challenges, and themes of simplicity in times of rapid changes. When told well, such narratives elicit sympathetic reactions and inspire followers, thus melding into the popular culture of a region or a country. Like the most prolific authors of *gauchesque* verse, Gutiérrez was a careful observer who transformed what he heard and saw into material for his narratives. While the *gauchesque* tradition had primed the atmosphere for *Juan Moreira*, Gutiérrez's evocation of two other aspects of popular culture—music and dance, on the one hand, and masculinity, on the other—also contributed to the narrative's appeal.

When thinking of music and dance in Argentina, the tango will immediately come to mind for many readers. But there were competing musical and dance traditions that preceded the tango. Many of these were especially significant in rural life throughout the Río de la Plata, and, because they were participatory, they were intimately related to expressions of nationalism and national identity. Take for example the *cielito*, the *media caña*, the *pericón*, and the *gato*. These similar square-dance-like forms were usually directed by a caller, whose voice rang out over the melodic guitars, and they included plenty of flirtation in addition to sung popular verse. When Moreira struck up a tune or showed his dance moves, the form was one of these country dances. He was also an accomplished *malambo* dancer, as Gutiérrez tells us. Another country dance, the malambo was a show of virtuosity. It consisted of lightening-fast leg movements, including plenty of boot stomping and "scrubbing" the dance floor with foot sweeps, and thus was a real crowd pleaser. Today visitors to Argentina can glimpse a malambo on outings to estancias or even at fancier dinner theater shows in the heart of Buenos Aires. In the mid-1880s, when Moreira's story arrived at the circus and on the theater stage, the gato and the pericón occupied a central place in the program and drew enthusiastic applause. Cielitos, gatos, and pericones featured in the *gauchesque*, too, and they were danced literally everywhere. So when Gutiérrez described music and dance scenes, he was presenting a popular cultural practice that resonated among readers, for they were moving to Argentina's (and Uruguay's) "national rhythms" before the tango took over this title.[5]

From cameos in *gauchesque* poetry to explosively applauded acts at the circus and crowd pleasers at tourist estancias, musical skill and dexterity on the dance floor were also displays of masculinity. Or, more accurately, they helped define the parameters of masculinity. "Scrubbing off" an impressive malambo is one way Moreira demonstrates his masculinity, and his skill (or that of other men) with a knife no doubt struck the manly chord with readers and spectators. But there are more subtle, yet equally important actions in Gutiérrez's narrative that illustrate the making and meaning of masculinity in the popular culture of late 1800s Argentina.

To begin, and let's just get it out in the open, Gutiérrez presents readers with a "bromance" between Moreira and his gaucho pal, Julián. Far

---

5. John Charles Chasteen, *National Rhythms, African Roots: The Deep History of Latin American Popular Dance* (Albuquerque: University of New Mexico Press, 2004); on contra dances in the Río de la Plata, see pp. 149–54.

from suggesting homosexual overtones, however, this relationship lends emotional depth to the characters as they stand together to face wrongdoing—certainly a "manly" position. There are plenty of tears shed, too, over the course of Moreira's misadventures. Yet these tears aim to appeal to readers' sense of empathy with men engaged in repeated violent confrontations. Then there is the fact that Moreira cannot return to the side of his beloved Vicenta, even though he has multiple opportunities to do so. No matter that Vicenta "deceived" him through no fault of her own, having moved in with one of the gaucho's compadres after being told that Moreira was dead. Going back to Vicenta would wound Moreira's sense of honor, which he seeks to avenge.

Another mode of behavior that defines masculinity toward the end of the century, and that in many respects is still central to the meaning of masculinity in Argentina (and Uruguay) today, is displaying *viveza criolla*. Roughly translated into English as cunning, or the skill with which one can deceive or take advantage of others, we see Moreira demonstrate repeatedly his viveza criolla—cheating the Indian chief Coliqueo and his men at the card table and pulling a fast one on Rico Romero at billiards are just two examples. From the perspective of twenty-first-century readers in the United States, these scenes are not flattering to our protagonist, but we can deduce that this skill elicited admiration from Moreira's peers. The men watching the pool game appreciated his ability to cheat Romero. And while Coliqueo and company did not appreciate in the least Moreira's deception, readers see clearly that this was a tactic Moreira had cultivated and used before. In fact, cheating at cards was "normal" and even expected among Moreira and his fellow card players at pulperías or around campfires. The skill with which one cheated others was a mark of liveliness and intelligence, and from there it was linked to the meaning of masculinity.

In many ways, then, *Juan Moreira* exemplifies the first definition of popular culture: it embodies the ideas, attitudes, and customs of the common people, especially in the nineteenth century. The book equally exemplifies a second definition of popular culture, more important in the twentieth century. Popular culture is mass produced and massively consumed. This modern popular culture, we can call it, is precisely what developed in late nineteenth-century Argentina, and *Juan Moreira* was the spark for its development. From the early 1880s through 1910, *Juan Moreira* jumped from one form of media to another, which guaranteed its widespread reception and fomented the formation of *moreirismo*. Moreirismo was a phenomenon consisting of publications that imitated Gutiérrez's narrative, employed Moreira as a character, or followed threads in the story. A sort of Moreira fan base (predominantly male) emerged, and a series of melodramas promoted the "myth of Moreira."

This myth gathered momentum in 1884 when Gutiérrez adapted *Juan Moreira* as a pantomime for the Podestá circus family, led by José Podestá. The Podestás were from Uruguay and already had an established reputation in Buenos Aires when they teamed up with the renowned Carlo Brothers (a U.S. equestrian and acrobatic troupe who enjoyed years of success in the Río de la Plata) to perform the *Moreira* drama as part of their circus. This "silent" *Moreira*, with the exception of music and song, was an immediate success. Two years later José Podestá added brief dialogue to the Gutiérrez adaptation of the play, which the family debuted as part of their circus show in April 1886. This new version of *Moreira* ushered in the Creole drama movement. Audiences embraced Creole dramas and their local color, for these represented tradition and modernity at once, which was exactly what Argentines, Uruguayans, and hundreds of thousands of European immigrants were living at the end of the 1800s.

Scenes from an early performance of the Creole drama Juan Moreira.

Don Franscisco asking Moreira what he thinks his lies about Sardetti will get him. *Instituto Nacional de Estudios de Teatro*, Buenos Aires, Argentina.

Moreira confronts Sardetti. *Instituto Nacional de Estudios de Teatro*, Buenos Aires, Argentina.

Moreira begs Julián to tell him the news of Vicenta and Juancito. *Instituto Nacional de Estudios de Teatro*, Buenos Aires, Argentina.

The Podestás and other traveling circus troupes performed the Creole drama *Juan Moreira* under makeshift tents in the countryside of southern Brazil, Uruguay, and Argentina as well as in Montevideo and Buenos Aires. Crowds filled the stands day after day to "pay homage to the cult of bravery," keeping circus troupes in town for weeks or months at a time before they pulled up stakes to move to their next venue.[6] So successful was the Creole drama *Juan Moreira* that it triggered the production of a series of dramas based on other notable gauchos and Gutiérrez texts. Stories of Santos Vega, Juan Cuello, Martín Fierro, amid other gaucho legends, all became Creole dramas, and the main protagonists were all larger-than-life characters. Vibrations of nationalism ran deep in these dramas, and performers as well as playwrights and impresarios were aware of the selling power of staged frontier experiences. But they also capitalized on the power of play, laughter, and the spectacular, be it in the form of the latest optical illusion or acrobatic stunt that entertained audiences prior to the main act, the Creole drama. Furthermore, Creole circus shows were family affairs, where there were children actors and sideshows for children in attendance. There was even a toned-down version of *Moreira* with all children actors!

From the circus the Moreira story spread and the myth of Moreira grew. The Podestás and other groups took their performance of *Moreira* to prestigious urban theaters in the 1890s, and with the shift in venue came a whole new group of spectators, too, including dignitaries and celebrities of urban highlife. Tobacco makers launched Martín Fierro and Juan Moreira brand cigarettes, with each box containing a collector's card depicting scenes from the stories. Composer Arturo Berutti's opera *Pampa*, based on *Juan Moreira*, debuted in 1897. And around 1910 *Juan Moreira* was rendered for the silver screen as a silent film, the first of several twentieth-century cinematic versions of the story. Throughout the period stretching from 1880 to 1910 the number of Moreira sympathizers and wannabes increased, too. There are abundant press reports of circus spectators storming the stage to defend Moreira from the police and army forces that approached him from behind as he attempted to escape his favorite hangout, La Estrella. One writer recalled attending a performance of *Moreira* at the Rafetto Circus, where a young man jumped onto the stage to defend Moreira as authorities were closing in on the hero. The audience member pulled out his knife—a real one, in contrast to the props of the actors—which led Moreira's opponents to flee the stage while the crowd cheered wildly. The company had to start

---

6. José J. Podestá, *Medio siglo de farándula*, with a preliminary study by Osvaldo Pellettieri (Buenos Aires: Galerna; Instituto Nacional de Teatro, 2003), 52.

José Podestá dressed in his gaucho finery in 1917; dedicated to Elías Regules, author of Creole dramas and founder of the Regules Creole Society. *Sociedad Criolla Elías Regules*, Montevideo, Uruguay.

the scene from the beginning because of the disruption.[7] Police records detail knife fights that broke out after Creole drama shows, where some tough inevitably was "trying to be like Moreira." Authorities often had to be called in to impose order among the crowds purchasing tickets for *Moreira* and other Creole dramas. And there is even record of a handful of hardened criminals who changed their names simply to Moreira.

These multiple layers—print, stage, silver screen—made the famous gaucho into a true culture hero, too large for a single genre to contain in the twentieth century. And yet, Juan Moreira, the real man, was a very nineteenth-century sort of fellow.

---

7. Alvaro Yunque, "Estudio preliminar" to *Croquis y siluetas militares: escenas contemporáneas de nuestros campamentos*, by Eduardo Gutiérrez (Buenos Aires: Librería Hachette, n.d.), 36.

The final scene from *Juan Moreira*, complete with folding chairs. *Archivo General de la Nación*, Dpto. Doc. *Fotográficos*, Argentina.

Nineteenth-Century Argentina

Whether we're talking about the real man or the mythical character, we need some historical background to understand Juan Moreira. The narrative shows the outlaw Moreira struggling with representatives of the state, supporting candidates for office, and fighting Indians as well as dueling with his rivals. The project of state making was in full force across Latin America. In Argentina this project entailed expanding the frontier southward, thus engaging in constant conflict with frontier inhabitants. One-time president and architect of public education Domingo F. Sarmiento, the country's most famous nineteenth-century statesman, termed this process the conquest of "civilization" over "barbarism." In this dichotomy, gauchos represented barbarism. Having spent most of the decade of 1870 as a sergeant in Argentina's national army along frontier outposts, Gutiérrez saw the process and consequences of state building up close. He was also acutely aware of the machinations of the region's political culture, which revolved around patron–client relationships. Patronage and its influences as well as symbolic violence come into sharp focus in *Juan Moreira*, as does their intimate relationship to the rights of citizenship. The narrative also reflects the economic and demographic transformation of Argentina (and Uruguay) in the last third of the century, brought about by great waves of immigration and an export boom that tied the region's economy to international markets. Lastly, Gutiérrez was unwittingly part of a cultural revolution that swept the region beginning in the 1870s. Specifically, new national systems of public primary education resulted in a rapidly growing literate citizenry, for whose attention (and pocketbooks) publishers competed. Forms of everyday reading proliferated, one of the chief examples being folletines such as *Juan Moreira*. To see how all this emerged, let's quickly survey the history of Argentina.

At the outset of the 1800s, when a series of civil wars erupted across Spanish America and resulted in independent republics, the Río de la Plata was sparsely populated in comparison with the colonial metropoles of Mexico and Peru. The Spanish crown had recently designated the backwater port of Buenos Aires as the capital of a new viceroyalty in 1776 in hopes of shoring up Spanish power in the southern hemisphere. Set on the banks of the Plata River, Buenos Aires concentrated a growing number of merchants and did a booming contraband trade with Europe, serving as the entrepôt for Bolivian silver, hides, and tallow before these goods embarked on their Atlantic journey. But just outside the fortifications of the small city lay a vast cattle frontier that stretched for hundreds of miles to the north, west, and south. Here millions of head of cattle and horses ranged wild. It was on these pampas, too, where the region's cowboys—the gauchos—roamed freely, at times clashing and at times cavorting, with indigenous groups.

The new viceroyalty of the Río de la Plata, and its new capital, did not prevent the old Spanish empire from fragmenting. In fact, one of the early calls for self-governance in Spanish America came from Buenos Aires patricians in May 1810. Celebrated later as the May "revolution," the call led to the outbreak of the wars for independence that rocked the Río de la Plata for nearly a decade. It was in the wars that gauchos had their debut as a fearsome military force. The "shoddily clad, dark-skinned" native horsemen had somewhat of a rehearsal when they contributed to routing the "neatly dressed, lily white" British navy officers who had invaded Buenos Aires and Montevideo in 1806 and 1807.[8] During the wars for independence these men on horseback proved lethal. They were skilled with makeshift lances and accustomed to wielding knives in their daily work.

---

8. Mariquita Sánchez de Thompson, *Intimidad y política: diario, cartas y recuerdos*, edited and with a preliminary study by María Gabriela Mizraje (Buenos Aires: Adriana Hidalgo), 150–53.

They could also form an improvised army in record time. All that was needed was the signal from a *caudillo*—a charismatic military leader, often one of the most adroit horsemen, who provided protection, work, and food for rural inhabitants. Caudillos inspired "admiration, obedience, and even fear"; they were "culture heroes" who "promoted idealistic emulation."[9] Their clients, in exchange, pledged their loyalty in a bond that was hard to break unless the trust that informed this patron-client relationship was itself broken.

For the next half century, gauchos, gaucho soldiers, or *montoneras*, and caudillos played an increasingly central role in Argentina's evolving political culture and nation-building process, and logically so. Up through the 1850s much of the economy in the areas surrounding Buenos Aires and its smaller sister city of Montevideo depended on cattle and the labor to process hides, leather goods, jerked beef, and animal fats for both local consumption and export. Gauchos provided much of the workforce in this economy, though they constituted a small fraction of landholders. Landowners, in contrast, tended to be wealthy and were often politicians or connected to political circles. Land itself was a key to political power, which is why the provincial and incipient national governments doled out parcels to supporters and allies. Some landowners became memorable caudillos, like Juan Manuel de Rosas. In fact, nowhere in Argentine history is the link between land and political power better represented than in the figure of Rosas, paramount among nineteenth-century Latin America's caudillos, who was directly responsible for the death of Moreira's father, as the reader will see.

Rosas was born into a military family whose wealth sprang from the vast estates they owned, where the young Juan Manuel developed his skills with a lasso, the *bolas*, made of three tethered stones, and on horseback. Rosas became governor of Buenos Aires province in 1829, a post he held for the next two decades. These years were synonymous with civil wars between the conservative Federalists and the liberal Unitarians—Argentina's first political parties—and their counterparts in Uruguay. This clash between conservatives and liberals flared throughout nineteenth-century Spanish America, though perhaps not with the intensity seen in Argentina and Uruguay. As head of the Federalists and de facto ruler of Argentina during this

---

9. Ariel de la Fuente, *Children of Facundo: Caudillo and Gaucho Insurgency during the Argentine State-Formation Process (La Rioja, 1853–1870)* (Durham: Duke University Press, 2000), 115; John Charles Chasteen, *Heroes on Horseback: A Life and Times of the Last Gaucho Caudillos* (Albuquerque: University of New Mexico Press, 1995): 4.

period, Rosas exercised strong-arm rule, rewarding his supporters and punishing his political enemies. Official documents brandished the Federalist slogan "Death to the Savage, Filthy, Traitorous Unitarians." Unitarians waged a war of words, too. Take for example Domingo Sarmiento's diatribe *Facundo: Civilization and Barbarism*, with which many readers may be familiar, targeting Rosas' political philosophy and policies. Another Unitarian, Esteban Echeverría, equated life in Rosas' Buenos Aires with a slaughterhouse, depicting Rosas and his henchmen as barbarous gauchos in his story titled *The Slaughterhouse*. In spite of their attempts to produce overly vehement portrayals of Federalists as the enemy with no room for nuance, both Unitarian writers touched on two truths that would echo for decades to come.

   First, political and symbolic violence took on new levels of ferocity, as the Federalist slogan hints. From the wars for independence to the Drug War, symbolic violence has been one of the more gruesome features of political life across Latin America. Rosas employed a special shock force called the *mazorca* to carry out acts of violence for show, with the specific intention of intimidating and repressing. One of the characteristic signs of the mazorca in action, which they had taken from daily work in the countryside, was the *degüello*, or slitting of the throat from ear to ear. On the civil war battlefields of the Río de la Plata, the degüello was the cheap way of finishing off one's opponent (as opposed to using a firearm, when one was available). At the pulpería knife fights, the degüello was the right of the victor. When gauchos were rounded up into montoneras, they could expect to employ or be the victims of the degüello. And when this act was used on political enemies, euphemistically referred to as "playing the violin," its symbolism was clear. What began to come into focus, then, during the Rosas years, though neither Rosas nor his mazorca deserve the credit here, was the emergence of a group of specialists in violence. This group drew heavily from residents of the countryside. When provincial coffers ran low as a result of Buenos Aires not sharing customs revenues, poverty rose in the interior, and when poverty rose, private violence and the mobilization of people to deploy violence became increasingly embedded in political culture.[10] Moreover, following the defeat of Rosas in 1852, these specialists in violence for several decades continued to exercise critical roles in military confrontations as well as in repression. It was not until the end of the century

---

10. De la Fuente, *Children of Facundo*, especially chapter 1; Chasteen, *Heroes on Horseback*, chapter 9.

that the state consolidated its monopoly on violence through a well-equipped national army and police forces.

A second point from the Rosas years is that the very idea of civilization versus barbarism that Sarmiento and company promoted tirelessly points to an increasingly stark divide between the city and the countryside. By the mid-1800s Buenos Aires was Argentina's most populous city. Its denizens made up around 10 percent of the national population (close to 1.1 million), a proportion that socioeconomic modernization in the late 1800s exacerbated: by the end of the century the city had close to 700,000 residents, more than 20 percent of the nation's total population. Beyond the numbers, though, was a mode of thinking that privileged the city in general as the apex of social organization. Cities harbored culture, went the idea. Their residents attended schools and were forced by the very proximity of social contact in urban spaces to develop "civilized" manners. And, as Sarmiento formulated in his *Facundo*, cities were the very opposite of the barren countryside, where schools were few and far between, where children were wont to participate in ruffian activities like horse racing and throwing the *taba*, and where violence was a way of life. Such rural deserts were simply ungovernable, according to many a Unitarian. Cities needed to be built in these areas, and people needed to populate them. The outcome of the push to develop rural Argentina ultimately did not turn out the way Sarmiento and many others had dreamed, as we will see. Two components of the effort to resolve the philosophical and physical city-countryside divide, however, transformed the course of Argentine history: the expansion of the frontier and the decades-long state sponsorship of immigration to Argentine (and Uruguayan) shores.

The impulse to expand the frontier, followed by settlement or patrolling of newly conquered lands, began under Rosas. Landholders, of course, saw economic opportunities in the open plains north, south, and west of Buenos Aires. This was prime grazing country, after all, where cattle could multiply ad infinitum and sheep could roam at will. The Buenos Aires government negotiated with some indigenous groups in the 1830s to allow new settlements in Indian territories, but the expansion of the frontier was by and large a military affair that lasted more than half a century, and it was one in which peasants who had been conscripted played a major role (often lamented as cannon fodder). The culmination of the expansion was the infamous series of sorties called the "Conquest of the Desert" in 1879, which provided new agricultural lands as well as room for the city of Buenos Aires to grow. This feature of Argentine history is much more in line with the U.S. experience of westward expansion during the nineteenth century than with the histories of most other Latin American nations. Frontier expansion was state making in progress. It was about the control of space. Armies carried out the confrontations to clear new lands. Yet once the military work had been completed, the Justice of the Peace or his assistants represented the otherwise not-very-present state on the vast, open pampa. They resolved disputes, sanctioned marriage, fulfilled a policing function, and communicated or carried out state policies. In a word, these figures were "the law," and they take on crucial roles in *Juan Moreira*, in part because of their responsibility in pushing Moreira down the "slippery slope" of crime but also because they illustrate the conflictual relationship of the state along the frontier.

In Gutiérrez's narrative as well as in the daily struggles rural residents faced in 1800s Argentina, these officers of the state were the arbiters of the rights of citizenship. From the wars for independence into the early twentieth century, the meaning of citizenship was an evolving concept in Argentina as well as throughout the rest of Latin America. Similarly, the rights that we consider today to be at the very core of citizenship were far from being guaranteed in any universal way until long after Moreira's death. On the contrary, and as readers will see clearly in the narrative, many of the very representatives of the state who were supposed to protect rights of citizenship ended up abusing them. The extent of this abuse varied according to class and economic status (more well-to-do rural inhabitants, or landholders, were often exempt from such treatment or could buy their way out of trouble) as well as geographic location (rural isolation often prevented even the most lax oversight). Threatening to send gauchos to fight Indians and then following through with the threat, often to extract certain behaviors or political benefits, appears frequently associated with the office of Justice of the Peace. Of course not every Justice or Assistant Justice was a Don Francisco, eager to strip peasants of their livelihood. But even where trafficking in influence or corruption was absent, there was the ever-present patronage system that permeated social relations.

Perhaps more vividly than its urban counterpart, frontier life throws into relief relationships to the "architecture" of power. And patronage was about power. On the pampa, gauchos and ranch hands often depended on patrons for food, protection, work, godfathers for their children, and small plots of land where they could live and grow a few crops. In exchange, patrons counted on these clients' loyalty, their service, and a body of men who could saddle up for battle or to make their presence felt at a polling station at the patron's order. There was also an emotional bond between patrons and clients that cannot be underestimated. This emotional connection stemmed from experiences patrons shared with clients, from admiration clients showed their patrons, and from a more generalized camaraderie. Some patrons became caudillos, and these provided a full-blown example of the give-and-take hierarchy that mobilized gauchos and political allies for decades. The patron-client relationship developed on smaller scales, too. Justices of the Peace cultivated their clients as did small-fry landowners. The personal magnetism that surrounds Juan Moreira wherever he goes and the ever-increasing number of supporters he has (or who fear him) as he flees his destiny present a wonderful portrait of the personal, clientelistic, and emotional components that underpinned patronage and the broader phenomenon of *caudillismo*. Gutiérrez himself sensed something of this magnetism when he met Moreira in 1874. In this sense, as readers make their way through *Juan Moreira*, they might consider what the narrative illustrates about the culture of rural Argentines who celebrated Moreira and what moral ideas the protagonist represents.

Patronage played out in another arena visible on the frontier, as well as in urban settings, and as backdrop to several of *Juan Moreira*'s most memorable scenes—elections. While relatively few eligible voters exercised their right throughout the 1800s, elections nevertheless conveyed important symbolic value as displays of state building and political power. Polling stations were usually set up near or in churches for citizens to "meet their electoral obligation under God's supreme protection."[11] Election sites could devolve into settings of intense violence or intimidation, as Gutiérrez recounts in *Juan Moreira*. Gutiérrez's narrative also does well to draw our attention to the collective atmosphere and act of voting. One did not want to be caught voting for the wrong candidate, especially when Moreira had anything to say in the matter as an electoral caudillo. Here, then, we had a specialist in violence who patrolled elections for his patron and who, in turn, could convince (or intimidate) others to vote with him—a forceful image of patronage. Parish and political clubs that emerged in the 1860s and 1870s mobilized voters in many of the same ways caudillos and powerful patrons helped to get out the vote. In addition to providing a social network for their members, these clubs took on tasks such as registering voters, organizing meetings, and overseeing

---

11. Quoted in Hilda Sábato, *The Many and the Few: Political Participation in Republican Buenos Aires* (Stanford: Stanford University Press, 2001), 56.

polling stations on election days. *Coimas* (bribes) often encouraged club or election officials to turn a blind eye or contest a result as needed, with the level of vehemence corresponding to the amount of the bribe.

Elections in frontier towns and frontier life more generally underwent radical changes in the last third of the nineteenth century as a result of an export boom that linked forevermore the Argentine economy to the world economy. Beginning in the 1870s Argentine exports, led first by wool and then agricultural products, found new markets in Britain and, to a lesser extent, in other Western European countries. British investors were the driving force behind major foreign investment in Argentine infrastructure projects, from telegraph and streetcar lines in cities, to Buenos Aires' new, modern port, to rail lines that fanned out from Buenos Aires to the countryside. The railroad—that hallmark of modernization—developed at an astounding pace and set in motion a transformation of the rural economy to center heavily on the cultivation of cereals. When the first trains started rolling in the late 1850s, they did so on five miles of track; in 1895, when the second national census was held, there were nearly nine thousand miles of rail lines; and by 1914, when exports slowed drastically, trains moved goods over twenty thousand miles of railways. As these lines made their way across the pampas and into sleepy frontier towns, they deposited imported manufactured goods and returned to port cities along the Plata River full of wheat, barley, and oats. In fact, by 1900 Argentina had emerged as one of the world's leading producers of wheat. The expansion of agricultural activity on the pampa physically changed the landscape, most notably by fencing off areas. This new mode of demarcating territory, not to mention the way rail lines split land, limited the movement of both cattle and gauchos, and it reduced drastically the amount of labor needed to manage herds.

So while the export bonanza resulted in a stream of profits that fed the construction of opulent cityscapes and the development of modern infrastructure, it had its negative consequences, too, including the shake-up of the rural economy. Around the turn of the century, cattle products, most importantly beef that could now be chilled or frozen for export, reentered the economy. But the export boom spiraled into depression and bust—which happened on several occasions from 1870 to 1914—when the global economy slowed or when foreign investors hesitated to pump more money into Argentina or demanded returns that the Argentine government could not guarantee. Put differently, the export boon was based on a neocolonial relationship, with the few winners being the foreign investors who owned rail-roads, tramways, and telegraph lines or the Argentine oligarchs who reaped export earnings. Such a setup was a prime target for protectionists and antimodernists, who in the Argentina of the late 1800s often blamed European immigrants for problems they identified with modernization.[12]

Immigration went hand in hand with an export boom and a reconfiguration of the rural economy, and the arrival of immigrants to Argentina (and Uruguay) is no doubt one of the distinguishing features of its history in the broader context of Latin America. Liberals, among them Sarmiento and Nicolás Avellaneda (who figures in *Juan Moreira* and who served as president in the 1870s), had long called for immigrants to bring civilization to "wild" Argentina. They envisioned Northern Europeans (from France, Germany, and England) settling in Argentina and instilling a Protestant work ethic in addition to populating the countryside. Beginning in the 1860s Congress sponsored official programs to attract European immigrants. Offices were established in Europe, and transatlantic passages were purchased for willing immigrants. The promise of social mobility and returning much wealthier to the homelands attracted immigrants. But both promoters of immigration and the immigrants who dreamed of better futures discovered that the reality was far from what they had hoped. Rather than the "civilized" (and light-skinned) Northern Europeans, Italians flocked to Argentina, followed closely in numbers by Spaniards, groups who because of economic conditions in their home countries were drawn to "hacer la América," literally "to do America." And come they did: from 1870 to 1914 close to six million immigrants poured into Argentina, with roughly half of these remaining permanently. In 1869 (the year of Argentina's first national census) immigrants accounted for around a third of Buenos Aires' population and just over 10 percent of the national total; by the end of the century most of the city's population had been born outside Argentina while immigrants made up a quarter of the nation's residents. It is no exaggeration to say that this period of immigration completely altered the region's demography.

Some immigrant groups worked in sheepherding, while a much larger number formed agricultural colonies in the provinces of Santa Fe,

12. Jeane Delaney, "Making Sense of Modernity: Changing Attitudes toward the Immigrant and the Gaucho in Turn-of-the-Century Argentina." *Comparative Studies in Society and History* 38, no. 3 (1996): 434–59.

Entre Ríos, Córdoba, and Buenos Aires. Many others settled in
the city of Buenos Aires (and smaller port cities such as Rosario),
literally building the new urban infrastructure with its Parisian-style
boulevards and monolithic buildings that give the city its European
architectural feel, laying the rail lines, building the new port, and populating the city's tenement houses. Immigrants owned industries and
stores, from pulperías to the finest tailoring shops. They contributed to
new forms of association in Argentina through their mutual aid
societies, immigrant community hospitals, and participation in political movements. Newcomers, however, were reluctant to become
"naturalized" citizens, for they wanted to avoid conscription, which
was the proverbial sword held over gauchos' heads. And despite the
employment opportunities, immigrants faced challenges ranging from
poor living conditions to increasingly widespread discrimination. In
fact, toward the end of the 1800s the original proponents of mass
immigration had reversed their position. There was a growing tendency to associate immigrants with an uptick in materialism and crime.
In addition, the rise in new professions linked to the export boom,
such as speculators, investors, and wholesalers, fueled a suspicious look
at how money was made, with immigrants again viewed as outsiders.
An idyllic countryside juxtaposed with changing cityscapes and the
values of the gaucho now no longer roaming free (except in people's
imaginations) but still an icon of a simpler time attracted sympathizers
around the turn of the century. The rapid influx of immigrants and
the socioeconomic modernization that accompanied the export boom
(and bust) generated the perfect climate for feelings of nativism and
nationalism to flourish.

One of the prime areas for the cultivation of nationalism, and one
that was the final building block of the state-making project, was
public primary education. A thriving public education system had
been one of Sarmiento's lifelong dreams. He had toured elementary
schools in Germany, France, and England in the 1840s, and two
decades later he visited the United States with his Uruguayan counterpart José Pedro Varela to meet Horace Mann and learn about
public education in New England. Upon returning to the Río de la
Plata, Sarmiento and Varela promoted legislation that in the 1870s
and 1880s established normal schools to train teachers and created
the first national compulsory public primary education systems in
both Argentina and Uruguay. By the end of the 1800s, public education in the region had become the most successful in Latin America.
Thousands of schools across both Argentina and Uruguay taught

hundreds of thousands of children, many from immigrant families, lessons in patriotism; literacy rates in these two countries were by far the highest in Latin America; and new generations of literate citizens joined the workforce and were thirsty for reading material. This massive reading public was not lost on publishers. At the end of the 1800s a thriving textbook industry produced texts and class notebooks for students, while newspaper, magazine, and book publishers competed for consumers. There was a flood of everyday reading material, which included illustrated magazines, posters lining streets, consumer products and their large-scale advertising campaigns in print, and Eduardo Gutiérrez's *Juan Moreira*.

The regional success story of education exemplifies a final point in this historical survey that should be coming into focus: Uruguay and Argentina shared similar, and often the same, histories up through the early twentieth century. To be sure, Juan Moreira was an Argentine gaucho who lived and died in the Argentine countryside. And Gutiérrez's *Juan Moreira* circulated first in Argentina. But Moreira's exploits and Gutiérrez's narrative quickly began to have an impact in Uruguay, and now it should be clear why. The historical forces that transformed the Argentine countryside and that fueled urbanization operated in the same ways in Uruguay. Rural residents there felt the same pressures as their Argentine counterparts. Uruguayan caudillos were mirror images of these leaders in Argentina. And there were gaucho toughs in Uruguay who challenged the state and became legends in their own right. They just did not reach the same level of fame as *Juan Moreira*.

Between Fact and Fiction

Eduardo Gutiérrez could not have imagined, even in his most gaucho dreams, the extent of *Moreira*'s impact, despite the lucrative returns from the text, nor would he live to see *Moreira*'s legacy take flight. He was not in the habit of proofreading his drafts or correcting proofs before his stories went to press. He wrote in the moment, for the moment, with practical goals in mind. That he had published *Juan Moreira* and most of his other narratives as folletines in Buenos Aires newspapers was almost natural given the Gutiérrez family ties to the press. His brothers José María and Carlos both founded newspapers where Eduardo got his publishing feet wet as a teenager and where he later collaborated as an editor of literary sections. He spent most of the decade of 1870 in the army, posted along the frontier, where he participated in combat on several occasions and where he gathered material for much of his writing. At the end of the 1870s, Gutiérrez resigned from his army position. Then came his big break in *La Patria Argentina*, a new paper his brother José María had created that would publish in installments and later in book form Gutiérrez's most successful narratives.

Growing up, Gutiérrez was not one for formal study, and he was rumored not to be much of a reader. He left the Colegio Nacional (the prestigious institution that prepared middle- and upper-class young males for lives of influence and power) shortly after enrolling and preferred to roam the burgeoning Buenos Aires. Though he read French and Spanish serial novelists, Gutiérrez seemed to draw most on *Don Quixote* and the *gauchesque* tradition (Bartolomé Hidalgo, interestingly, was a distant relative of his).[13] His other main sources of inspiration were oral traditions, which flowed freely on the frontier, and the world around him, including crime.

Theft, swindling, political violence, and true crime (as in homicide) became subjects of his texts, and these manifestations of crime are present at every turn in *Juan Moreira*. Crime is *the* great driving force of the narrative, be it crime against Moreira or crimes he commits. Crime was one of the text's features that kept readers coming back to see how Moreira's fate would play out, how well he could exact justice, albeit through killing, or how criminal actions of authorities would end Moreira's plight. It was through Moreira's violent killing of the *pulpero* Sardetti, his deadly attacks on police forces and army officers, and, yes, what we may see as his ignoble criminal actions against Indians that his reputation for bravery and fierceness formed. Scarce police files recorded some of Moreira's alleged crimes—the murder of an *estanciero*, the wounds officers received from having attempted to apprehend him, the brutality of his work when rounding up support for his patron or intimidating voters on election days. Moreira operated outside the law, but he was not your typical bandit either. Argentine criminologists and men of letters qualified the "real-life" Moreira as a "ferocious, instinctive, natural-born criminal" and as "a repulsive, vulgar delinquent whose image was glorified on stage, and who became a subject of sincere admiration for our popular

---

13. Jorge B. Rivera, *Eduardo Gutiérrez* (Buenos Aires: Centro Editor de América Latina, 1967).

classes."[14] Then again, such men were not likely to find any redeeming qualities in the real Moreira or in Gutiérrez's portrayal. Gutiérrez took a more subtle approach to Moreira and crime, as readers will see. It was this narrated Moreira, and the Moreira of the Creole drama, who ultimately occupied a more prominent place in Argentina's social "imaginary."[15]

One could say that in *Juan Moreira* we can observe Eduardo Gutiérrez's skill at blurring the line between fact and fiction, which definitely helped pave the way for *Moreira*'s vigorous afterlife. This combination of fact and fiction is still part of the Moreira legacy. Visitors to the town of Lobos can glimpse a wooden plaque with the words "*Pulpería y casa de bailes* (dance hall) *La Estrella,*" where Moreira took his last stand, and see the cemetery where Moreira's bones most likely rest. But there are competing stories regarding the whereabouts of Moreira's skull (one of these points to it being located in Lobos, another in Luján), neither of which townspeople in the know believe to be very credible. Of course Gutiérrez took great pains to present his portrait of Moreira as a sort of social documentary in which real life is more extraordinary than the novelist's imagination. He was *not* writing fiction, as he reminds us repeatedly with asides relating to the "verifiable" evidence he pieced together, the interviews he did, the "scenes of Moreira's life" he visited, the time he saw Juan Moreira, and the anecdote he includes from a reader at the end of the text. We can question how Gutiérrez knew what Moreira was thinking at a given moment or the words he exchanged with friends and foes. And we can chuckle at what may come across as a picture of a superhuman gaucho.[16] Yet all this effort aimed to present a narrative of ornamented truth, a historical portrait in which mythical qualities combined with real life.

And Gutiérrez was a master at crafting that narrative. His writing style was straightforward; action and movement, more than description, populate the narrative; and he probed themes with which readers across social classes could identify, themes like corruption, clientelism, humor, violence, and hope. Many of these will resonate for twenty-first-century readers. We can also grasp the spirit of entertainment that

---

14. Nerio Rojas, *El diablo y la locura y otros ensayos* (Buenos Aires: Librería El Ateneo Editorial, 1951), 199–203; Eusebio Gómez, "La mala vida en Buenos Aires." *Archivos de psiquiatría y criminología aplicada a las ciencias afines: medicina legal, sociología, derecho, psicología, pedagogía*, año 7 (1907): 431–42.

15. Fabio Carrizo (José Alvarez) in *Caras y Caretas*, April 4, 1903, no. 235.

16. M.E.L., *Juan Moreira: realidad y mito* (Buenos Aires: n.p., 1956).

Eduardo Gutiérrez captured in the story. Gutiérrez composes incredibly cinematic scenes: the hero riding with the wind across the moonlit pampa; a somber Moreira improvising a tune to fellow gauchos; and his boldly cut figure, with lightening bolts coming out of his eyes in the dark night sky, confronting each batch of officers bent on taking him. Suspense and melodrama were likewise central to Gutiérrez's formula, and there's plenty of both in *Juan Moreira* to keep the adrenaline flowing. And then there are the passages that appealed to readers' sympathy, like when Moreira bids farewell to Vicenta and Juancito, in the image of crowds coming for hours to pay homage to Moreira's corpse (or verify that he was in fact dead), or with the final scene of Moreira's trusty dog Cacique mourning on his grave. Here we have a timeless tale of an underdog fighting for what is right, a figure who dared to stand up to the abuse of power, which struck sympathetic chords in the Río de la Plata.

No wonder, then, that readers in 1880 could not get enough of *Moreira*. Most readers today, however, won't regard Moreira as a hero. Moreira's thoughtless mistreatment of Indians is a prime example. Nineteenth-century Argentines espoused the same "scientific racism" that held sway in the United States. But sometimes it is hard to tell whether certain attitudes belonged to Moreira, the man, or Gutiérrez, the author. The author's relationship to the story he narrates may leave you pondering. What is certain, though, is that reading this fabulously popular book will enhance your understanding of many aspects of nineteenth-century Argentina and Uruguay, not least of which is how a knife-wielding gaucho outlaw became an enduring hero.

Enjoy the ride.

SUGGESTED READINGS

Acree, Jr., William G. *Everyday Reading: Print Culture and Collective Identity in the Río de la Plata, 1780–1910*. Nashville: Vanderbilt University Press, 2011.
> *A close look at the uses of reading and writing in daily life, including the gauchesque and their impacts on identity throughout Argentina and Uruguay.*

Baily, Samuel L. *Immigrants in the Lands of Promise: Italians in Buenos Aires and New York City, 1870–1914*. Ithaca: Cornell University Press, 1999.
> *A comparative study that reveals motivations for leaving the homeland as well as family networks, work opportunities, and challenges that shaped the migrant experience of Argentina's largest group of immigrants.*

Bethell, Leslie, ed. *Argentina since Independence*. New York: Cambridge University Press, 1993.
> *A collection of scholarly essays that treat major issues in Argentine political and economic history from the first postcolonial decades through the early twentieth century; see especially the first three chapters.*

Chasteen, John Charles. *Heroes on Horseback: A Life and Times of the Last Gaucho Caudillos*. Albuquerque: University of New Mexico Press, 1995.
> *A riveting exploration of caudillos as culture heroes and the collective sentiments they inspired.*

Dabove, Juan Pablo. *Nightmares of the Lettered City: Banditry and Literature in Latin America, 1816–1929*. Pittsburgh: University of Pittsburgh Press, 2007.
> *A panoramic tour of banditry in literature across Latin America; see in particular chapters 3 and 10.*

de la Fuente, Ariel. *Children of Facundo: Caudillo and Gaucho Insurgency during the Argentine State-Formation Process (La Rioja, 1853–1870)*. Durham: Duke University Press, 2000.
> *A detailed study of caudillos and the motivations rural inhabitants had for aligning with these charismatic leaders; one of the most magnetic caudillos*

in the area of Argentina in focus was El Chacho Peñaloza, about whom Gutiérrez wrote El Chacho, *another narrative blending fact and fiction.*

Halperín Donghi, Tulio, Iván Jaksic, Francine Masiello, and Gwen Kirkpatrick, eds. *Sarmiento, Author of a Nation.* Berkeley: University of California Press, 1994.
    A rich collection of essays that delve into the historical moment of Argentina's most famous nineteenth-century statesmen as well as the reach and reception of his writing, including the political diatribe Facundo.

Johnson, Lyman L., ed. *The Problem of Order in Changing Societies: Essays on Crime and Policing in Argentina and Uruguay, 1750–1940.* Albuquerque: University of New Mexico Press, 1990.
    This collection of essays presents urban and rural perspectives into the connections between crime, attempts to establish order, and social change; see particularly chapter 3 on knife dueling and honor.

Lynch, John. *Argentine Caudillo: Juan Manuel de Rosas.* Wilmington: SR Books, 2001.
    An engaging biographical portrait of the Río de la Plata's most powerful caudillo, with a nuanced analysis of the extent and limits of his authority.

———. *Caudillos in Spanish America, 1800–1850.* New York: Oxford University Press, 1992.
    A classic study of caudillos, their political power, and the sources of their influence from Mexico to Argentina.

Masiello, Francine R. *Between Civilization and Barbarism: Women, Nation, and Literary Culture in Modern Argentina.* Lincoln: University of Nebraska Press, 1992.
    This evocative book surveys the impacts women had on the process of nation formation and Argentine political culture, and considers their roles in the world of nineteenth-century letters; see especially parts 1 and 2.

Moya, José C. *Cousins and Strangers: Spanish Immigrants in Buenos Aires, 1850–1930.* Berkeley: University of California Press, 1997.
    A history of the complex stories of Spanish migrants to Argentina, the country's second largest group of immigrants; especially useful when read in tandem with Baily.

Rock, David R. *Argentina, 1516–1987: From Spanish Colonization to Alfonsín,* rev. ed. Berkeley: University of California Press, 1987.
    A thorough survey of Argentine history, useful as a reference to guide further examination of specific themes.

————. *State Building and Political Movements in Argentina, 1860–1916.* Stanford: Stanford University Press, 2002.
  An in-depth analysis of the complex process of state building, from the fall of caudillo power to the rise of political factionalism, in which gauchos, immigrants, and oligarchs all play a part.

Rodríguez, Julia. *Civilizing Argentina: Science, Medicine, and the Modern State.* Chapel Hill: University of North Carolina Press, 2006.
  A captivating study of the role science and medicine played in the politics of state building from the mid-1800s into the twentieth century.

Sábato, Hilda. *The Many and the Few: Political Participation in Republican Buenos Aires.* Stanford: Stanford University Press, 2001.
  A succinct history of the transformations in Buenos Aires political culture during the second half of the 1800s, with particular attention to the workings of elections, political mobilization, and the construction of a public sphere.

Scobie, James R. *Argentina: A City and a Nation,* 2nd ed. New York: Oxford University Press, 1971.
  Scobie's classic study of the conflicts between Buenos Aires (and the coast) and interior provinces underscores a major interpretive framework for understanding Argentine cultural, social, economic, and political history.

Shumway, Nicolas. *The Invention of Argentina.* Berkeley: University of California Press, 1991.
  An engaging exploration of nineteenth-century intellectual and literary circles and their intersection with political factions and variants of nationalism.

Slatta, Richard W. *Gauchos and the Vanishing Frontier.* Lincoln: University of Nebraska Press, 1992.
  A graceful narrative of the transformation of frontier society in Argentina and the accompanying impacts on gauchos and ranch hands over two centuries.

————, ed. *Bandidos: The Varieties of Latin American Banditry.* Westport: Greenwood Press, 1987.
  Saddle up with this collection of essays for an appraisal of how Moreira compares with other bandits and outlaws throughout Latin America.

Sorensen, Diana. *Facundo and the Construction of Argentine Culture.* Austin: University of Texas Press, 1996.
  This study of Sarmiento's Facundo *is a must read, not only for its innovative exploration of one of the pillars of Latin American literary, cultural, and political thought, but also for Sorensen's tour of nineteenth-century Argentina's literary and cultural landscapes.*

Map of Moreira's Movements.

The Gaucho Juan Moreira

i

Juan Moreira is one of those figures who stride into this world, into any walk of life, destined for celebrity, like a walking bronze statue. This gaucho was no twisted, cowardly, blood-thirsty criminal, as some have said.

No, Juan Moreira's instincts were gentle and noble and, had they been properly directed and educated, his life would have turned out differently. At the head of a regiment of cavalry, Moreira would have been a credit to his country, a national glory, but on the slippery slope of crime, viciously pursued and fighting for his life, he turned on his pursuers with heroic fury. The valor of the "bandit" Juan Moreira seems almost super-human, yet he was in most ways no different from most of our gauchos, strong of heart and generous of spirit.

Until the age of thirty he was a hard-working resident of Matanzas, a pampa neighborhood where he was generally held in high esteem, though he had only a flock of sheep and a few cattle. His specialty was breaking horses, and his neighbors brought him animals that nobody else could come near. No one had ever seen Juan Moreira drunk. He wasn't the sort of gaucho who wastes time drinking and gambling at the rural stores called *pulperías*. He took no part in the rowdy gatherings that normally ended in a fight, with another cross sprouting in the graveyard and another poor soul sent off to join an army unit on the southern frontier, where so many gauchos are sent as punishment, simply because, having lost their homes, they've become "vagrants," a crime punishable by forced conscription. But let's get back to Moreira, who only appeared at the pulpería on days when the whole neighborhood was there for big horse races. Quite a figure he cut, then, on his magnificent dappled bay horse, with saddle and bridle to match, gaucho finery.

The only time Moreira was known to draw blood was when an Indian raid struck nearby. On such occasions, they called up the national guard, and dutiful gauchos like Moreira put down lassos and branding irons and rallied around the local military commander. Moreira did not hesitate to take his best horses into the fight, during which he always distinguished himself, and after which he returned home without any thought of reward, considering that he had merely done his duty. He won a reputation for fleetness and bravery among his neighbors, who eventually considered that no attempt to control frontier Indians was likely to succeed without Moreira's participation.

Moreira lived happily married with a local girl, daughter of a poor but honest neighbor, and their little boy was his pride and joy. Aside from his wife, whom he idolized, he desired nothing more out of life. He never went to fight Indians without first squeezing little Juan tightly in his arms, and never returned without pulling the child up to the pommel of his saddle and taking him for a ride. Soon the little boy got a pony of his own, expressly trained by his father, who also lovingly braided the animal's bridle with a dexterity that few could equal. Then little Juan began to accompany his father, often, on little excursions to town or a friend's ranch.

Moreira also had several large, two-wheeled pampas carts and oxen to pull them. Much of what he earned came from the loads of hides, wool, and other local products that he carted to the train station on behalf of local ranchers. The landowners who entrusted him with their goods for sale never asked him for a receipt, much less payment in advance. Nobody for miles around had a better reputation among his neighbors than did Juan Moreira, whose word was his bond.

His neighbors also knew him, in earlier years, as a sort of roving troubadour or, as they would say, *payador*. Moreira had a fine voice, and when he tuned his guitar to sing at a country dance, surrounded by friends, he always impressed them with his tender lyrics, normally the ten-line *décimas* beloved by our gauchos. Such delicate sentiments are not rare among our gaucho troubadours, whose emotions fill the singers' dark, intelligent faces and go straight to their listeners' hearts. When a gaucho sings, his voice takes on a rare quality of sadness and yearning. In song the gaucho finds release from his long string of misfortunes, his eyes brighten with tears, and his feelings flow from fingers to guitar strings. A true payador of the pampas, like the famous Santos Vega, produces a sublime, other-worldly sound that completely enthralls the listener. All gauchos possess an artistic sensibility, however, and all play the guitar more or less by instinct, without any musical instruction whatsoever. Juan Moreira possessed these qualities in a high degree. When he began to play the guitar at a dance, the assembly fell silent, and his plaintive verses moved men and women alike.

I met Juan Moreira on only one occasion, in 1874, but I've never forgotten the sound of his voice. He was already being called a bandit, and his frightful reputation had already spread to small towns across the pampa. And yet, he had about him something so appealing, that anyone who met him had the same thought as I did: This man *cannot be* a bandit.

Nobility characterized his face, and also the way that he carried himself, and he spoke with profound sincerity, bathing the face of his interlocutor with the light of his sad, dark eyes. His handsome face was framed by a thick, black, curly mane that reached to his shoulders and by a silky, full beard, equally black, that reached his chest. His eyes were attractive, his nose aquiline, and his mouth wore a bitter smile. One sensed a powerful and attractive spirit.

Moreira was thirty-four years old at the time—tall, and not thin. His dress was the picturesque stuff that gauchos wear, more or less the national costume. Instead of trousers he wore a black wool *chiripá* and white cotton *calzoncillos* with fringe around the bottom, like a real old-time gaucho, and around his waist, the typical wide leather *tirador* decorated with silver coins. All his clothing was scrupulously clean, even his spotless white shirt. In addition to the chiripá and calzoncillos, the tirador supported two *trabucos*, old-fashioned short-barreled shotguns with wide, flaring bronze barrels and, thrust under it at the small of Moreira's back, within reach of his right hand, his *facón*, with its two-foot blade and silver handle, inlaid with gold. More gaucho finery. Add high boots and spurs (also of silver), a black jacket, a silk kerchief at his neck, and broad-brimmed hat. A silver-handled riding whip hung from the wrist of his right hand, and on the little finger shone a gemstone ring. Finally, across his chest on one side, a gold watch chain descended into a side pocket of his tirador.

This was the Juan Moreira about whose daring deeds the gauchos sing their melancholy airs. What powerful motive, what fatal force led this good, upstanding man—a moral exemplar until the age of thirty—to a life of crime? I have traveled to the scenes of Moreira's life to investigate directly, and I have not found evidence of any mean or cowardly act to sully the hero whose story I am about to tell, even toward the end, when he lived permanently on the run, pursued by every lawman on the pampa. As he said, there weren't enough lawmen in Buenos Aires province to take him prisoner, and he said it so often, that he knew the day they caught him would be his last.

An inquiry concerning the criminality of our countryside should start with the general picture, which is simple. Our gauchos have only two options, to become bandits, in the manner I will describe, or be drafted into the army as cannon fodder. Gauchos are routinely deprived of their civil rights and even, one could say, of their human rights. Both military and police authorities abuse our gauchos, who have no recourse, because if they resist, it's into the army and off to the southern frontier. Gauchos cannot find honorable work at all, and their crime? To be native sons and citizens of Argentina! No one wants to hire the native born when foreign laborers can be used instead. A landowner who hires gauchos will lose his workers for days at election time, when the Justice of the Peace and the local military commander herd them like sheep to the polling places, or for weeks or months, when the National Guard mobilizes to fight Indians, or for years, if he's been drafted into the army. Foreign workers neither vote nor serve in the armed forces, and their presence has made the gaucho a pariah in his own country.

The gaucho lives in horror of being drafted into the army, and with good reason. Off he goes to the army as punishment, and why? Because he can't find work, so he's called a vagrant. Or because the local military commander is angry (the gaucho voted for his employer's candidate, not the commander's) and won't give him papers. Or just because his wife is pretty and someone wants her, someone powerful. So off he goes to the frontier with shackles on his feet, like a common criminal, to suffer two years of enlisted misery, without adequate food or clothing, receiving horrible treatment. He counts himself lucky if, at the end of his two years, he gets discharged as promised. Back home he rides, hoping to forget his suffering in the quiet of his humble little house on the pampa, in the company of his cherished wife and children.

But it's at home, precisely, that the worst awaits him. His horses, all his animals, are gone, taken and divided up by whoever ransacked his house. His wife now lives with the someone powerful who wanted her and who had sent him to the army in shackles to get her. It's not her fault. She had no other choice, poor thing, if she were not to starve. And his children? They've been given out as servants to various families, committed to serve them for God knows how long. The gaucho's heart overflows with pain and shame as he contemplates the desolation of everything he loves. It overflows, and then absorbs the venom and hate that have been poured over him by this awful wrong. He wants revenge, and gets it, which makes him an outlaw, pursued night and day. He'll never stop fleeing and he'll fight to the death, because if he surrenders he'll still be "killed resisting arrest" on the official report.

The authority who did him such great harm, a local Justice, for example, lives in fear that the gaucho will come some night to settle accounts, and he'll try anything to escape the gaucho's vengeance, which is a sure thing, sooner or later. Meanwhile, the miserable outlaw lives on the run, stealing to be able to eat, killing to defend himself and, eventually, killing out of habit, and even, in the fullness of time, killing for pleasure. Life on the run has driven him to drink, and to acquire all the other vices that go along with it.

This is how a good man, such as Juan Moreira, becomes a criminal. What right do we have to condemn him? And yet, our prisons are full of men like this, not born to a life of crime but forced into it, eventually suffering the ultimate punishment with courage and serenity. Such, in general outline, horrible but undeniable, is the destiny of our gauchos.

Let us turn, now, to the particular case at hand. To understand why Juan Moreira became an outlaw, we must go back ten years to a happier time, before anyone ever felt the sharp point of his facón.

ii

Moreira grew up in the pampa neighborhood of Matanzas. He never knew his father, who was also a famous man. Readers may remember, and may even have met, a certain much-feared Moreira to whom the dictator Rosas gave a sealed message to deliver, a message that said, "Shoot the bearer of this message." That was the unfortunate father of our hero.

We've already seen that, like most gauchos, our hero played the guitar and sang décimas. On the serene moonlit nights of his youth, young Moreira would saddle his dappled bay horse, tie his guitar behind the saddle, and ride to the house of a friend, where he was always welcome because his arrival promised gaiety and dancing. Friends and neighbors gathered at the house with high expectations, passing the mate gourd and gin bottle around, a sip of mate, a shot of gin, as they listened with rapt attention to Moreira's song. Then the dancing started and continued until midnight or one o'clock in the morning.

It was at a party like this that he met Vicenta, a young woman whose beauty was proverbial in Matanzas. After that, Moreira took his guitar most often to Vicenta's house. Everyone always had a good time at these parties, which passed without the slightest trouble of the kind that sometimes occurs, because just as Moreira was well liked, he was also well respected. Nobody in Matanzas wanted to make an enemy of Juan Moreira, and besides, parties at the house of an honorable family seldom end in a ruckus. The guests are hard-working folk, neighbors, and possibly a traveling stranger or two who has been invited to unsaddle and spend the night, because our gauchos consider hospitality a sacred obligation. Outlaws, drifters, and other dangerous men stay away from parties like this and gravitate instead to isolated pulperías, where they arrive under cover of darkness and leave early the next morning. The parties at Vicenta's house were attended, in addition, by the local Assistant Justice of the Peace and by a wealthy merchant or two whom Vicenta or Moreira counted as friends.

Moreira loved Vicenta the way a gaucho loves, with primitive innocence, without a word, revealing the feelings of his virgin heart in the gaze of his magnificent eyes and in the mumbled "This one's for you," with which he dedicated his most fervent décimas. Vicenta understood, of course, just as silently, and confirmed her acceptance of his love by the way she met his gaze with her own and served his mate lightly sprinkled with cinnamon. Moreira was quite a catch— brave and handsome, all the girls sighed when he sang—and Vicenta's father shared her enthusiasm. In addition to everything else, Moreira was an honest, hard-working man, with a modest patrimony that, in the right hands, would be more than enough to take care of Vicenta. Therefore her father encouraged the match and wanted to see the couple properly married as soon as possible.

The Assistant Justice who came to Vicenta's parties had been after her for some time, with intentions quite different from those of Moreira. He looked negatively, indeed, on Moreira's courtship of the girl, which thwarted his plans of seduction. Moreira was too attractive and capable to defeat in fair competition, which, anyway, had never entered the mind of the Assistant Justice. Very quickly, he began the machinations that our rural authorities employ to harass their enemies for whatever cause, the machinations that end with shackles and forced induction into the army. Moreira did not suspect the other's perfidy, however, and all went on as before. He would not be easy prey, this man of unblemished virtue. Moreira's business dealings thrived, and soon he was lending Sardetti, owner of a nearby pulpería, ten thousand pesos that Sardetti needed to buy some loads of wool and hides. The loan was made with a handshake and nothing written down.

And at about that time, Moreira finally opened his mouth to ask for Vicenta's hand in marriage with her father's blessing, which was happily given. In one month, they were married.

That was a memorable celebration, with fancy liquor and hot fried pies, and everybody danced all night, got totally "worn out," as they say, and at sun-up, the guitar was still ringing. That same night came the first act of hostility from the Assistant Justice, who did not attend the party and, the next day, sent a deputy to collect five hundred pesos from Moreira for having given a party without official permission. His father-in-law was against it, but Moreira, to conserve his new happiness, paid the money, laughing that this must be a hazing for newlyweds, because he considered Francisco (the Assistant Justice's name) to be his friend.

The "hazing" continued, though, another fine and another, getting the notice of Moreira's neighbors, who knew that this did not bode well. Sometimes cattle or horses get into people's crops, it's common, but one day the Justice called Moreira to his house to humiliate the gaucho because of a stray animal. Another fine. Moreira paid obediently, but under protest. The next fine was for not reporting to the house of the Assistant Justice when called yet again, after he and Vicenta had a party, to pay another fine for disturbing the peace.

Moreira's mood turned increasingly sour, until one day he decided to go ask his "friend" Francisco why he was being persecuted. The Assistant Justice listened to the gaucho's just grievance, but replied that he had nothing to explain. If Moreira didn't watch his step, he'd have shackles on his feet. Moreira turned pale when he heard those words, but he answered with composure.

"I haven't offended anyone, Justice Francisco. You are after me, that's all, and that will not end well."

"Is that a threat?" asked the Assistant Justice, raising his voice. "Then you're going to the stocks, right now!"

Let me describe the venerable institution called "the stocks" used by officials of the Justice of the Peace as routine punishment in the distant and forgotten towns of the pampa. A slab of heavy *ñandubay* wood is drilled with holes the size of a man's neck and wrists and then sawn in two horizontally through the holes. With a hinge at one end and a lock at the other, the two halves can be closed around the prisoner's neck and wrists or perhaps his ankles, keeping him painfully "stock still" for as long as the punishment lasts. Moreira's "friend" Francisco ordered forty-eight hours. This instrument of torture, formerly employed by the Spanish Inquisition and now by the Republic

of Argentina, is placed outside under a tree, the prisoner's only protection against the elements. Moreira was there for two days and
two nights without uttering the slightest complaint, a stoicism that
annoyed the Justice of the Peace, so much so, that he did not even
allow Vicenta to spend the night at her husband's side, the only sort of
protest usually permitted. The numerous friends who wanted to visit
Moreira in the stocks were sent away as well.

When he was finally released, Moreira went home, saddled his
dappled bay horse, and rode to the house of his good friend, Giménez,
the best man at his wedding, to whom he explained the situation,
asking for advice. He had no wish to lose everything in a senseless
conflict with the likes of the Assistant Justice. Giménez advised him to
go straight to the Justice of the Peace himself, protesting the outrage.
Unfortunately, the Assistant Justice got there first, and he told his
superior a pack of lies about Moreira's behavior. Why, the insolent
devil had gone so far as to threaten him in his own house! So the gaucho rode to town and went before the Justice of the Peace to invoke
his rights, but what gaucho has rights?

The gaucho demanded that justice be done, but the Justice turned
a deaf ear. The gaucho protested that all his neighbors could testify
about his good conduct and reputation. At that, he was thrown out of
the office, given "one last chance."

· · ·
iii

Juan Moreira left the office of the Justice of the Peace with the seed
of a desire in his heart—a desire for vengeance that would grow and
grow. He was beginning to see that he had no rights that his strong
arm did not win, nor any hope of justice without his knife in hand. He
rode home with a shadow of unshakable resolve on his brow. When
his neighbors, astonished by Moreira's patience and forbearance, told
him not to let that cur Francisco treat him like a helpless child, the
gaucho assured them that he would tolerate nothing more. And from
that day forward, Moreira put aside the knife that he normally carried

for work, thrust under his tirador at the small of his back, and in its place he carried his razor-sharp two-foot facón, with its silver handle inlaid with gold.

Several months passed without further incident. The effect of the past ugliness began to fade, and cheerfulness returned to Moreira's humble abode. Authorities in the provincial capital appointed a new Justice of the Peace for Matanzas, although most of the Assistant Justices, including the gaucho's erstwhile friend Francisco, remained in place. Moreira's enemy seemed to have changed tactics or, perhaps, reconsidered the risks of persecuting our hero.

At that point, Moreira's son was born and became the center of his world. The fancy facón disappeared to make way for his working knife, and the gaucho's old high spirits returned fully. Vicenta's parties, with Juan on guitar, became the talk of the neighborhood again. The Assistant Justice sent emissaries to explain that he was so, so sorry about what had happened and that he wanted to make a fresh start. We've seen, already, Moreira's great generosity of spirit. He had never been the sort to brood or hold a grudge. So he went personally to shake Francisco's hand and invite him to the baptism of his son the following Saturday.

Saturday was a happy day for the whole neighborhood. The proud parents went all out and roasted a whole steer over an open fire. There was mate and liquor to drink and a whole slew of guitar players, because each of the gaucho's friends had brought his own, eager to celebrate the baptism of little Juancito Moreira. The gaucho's face was radiant with the happiness that Juancito's birth had brought, nothing less than his own spiritual rebirth after the terrible trials he'd endured. His ecstatic singing and guitar work reached their apogee some time past midnight, when the new father "scrubbed off" a fast *malambo* (as the colorful expression goes) amid the most frenetic applause. Moreira drank too much that night, which only resulted in greater hilarity, because those who knew him all say that he was happiest and most playful when he'd "had a few." The party lasted for two whole nights, including the day between, and the collective enthusiasm never flagged. When a guest started seeing double and was unable to dance he went to sleep it off in the high grass and, when he woke up, returned to the party. Such was the baptismal celebration of Juancito, which took on mythic proportions in the neighborhood, and the rebirth of his father, who then went back to work, harder than ever, to construct a bright future for his son.

The end of Moreira's truce with the Assistant Justice was announced by a string of niggling hassles and then a four hundred peso fine because two of his cows had gotten into a wheat field and done minor damage. Moreira turned white with rage when Francisco announced the cause and amount of the fine. His right hand moved imperceptibly toward the handle of his knife, but just then an image of little Juancito passed before his eyes, and he restrained himself. He paid the fine, and left the house of the Assistant Justice, feeling again the desire for vengeance whose seed had been planted some time before. The desire was growing. It made him taciturn that evening as he sat with his little family, braiding the reins that Juancito, barely walking, was nonetheless ready to start using on his pony. Vicenta, who sat at his side, combing the gaucho's long black curls, had lost her girlish figure in the fullness of motherhood and was now a woman grown, more beautiful than ever.

Moreira heard of a business opportunity, about that time, and he asked his friend Sardetti for the ten thousand pesos he'd lent him a year earlier. Sardetti asked for a little more time because business had been bad, and Moreira readily granted it, only requesting that Sardetti pay him back as soon as possible. Two months passed, the merchant asking always for more time because he simply didn't have the cash. Little by little the gaucho ran out of patience, and he finally told Sardetti that if he weren't repaid soon he'd have to sue. The repayment didn't happen and Moreira lodged a complaint with his old friend Francisco, who ordered that Sardetti appear before him. The merchant and the Assistant Justice may have arranged everything in advance, or possibly Sardetti was improvising in bad faith. The fact is, though, that in the presence of Moreira the merchant denied that there was any debt at all. He had received no money from the gaucho and didn't owe him a single peso. The Assistant Justice turned to Moreira:

"What do you think your lies will get you?" he sneered. "Why do you demand money that nobody owes you?"

"All I want is what belongs to me," said Moreira, trembling with fury, "and I want it because I *need* it. When this man denies his debt, he robs me, and I've come to demand justice."

"I'll give you justice, fool, for lying like a dog."

Moreira's right hand reached reflexively for his knife, without finding it. He'd taken the precaution of leaving it at home when he came to the house of the Assistant Justice. He stood silent for an instant, then spoke with an eerie calm.

"So, you don't owe me a thing, you say?" he asked Sardetti, who paled but answered dryly:

"Nothing."

Moreira turned to the Assistant Justice.

"And you refuse to make him pay?"

"Obviously, given that there is no debt, only your miserable attempt to cheat an honest merchant."

Moreira fixed his dark eyes on Sardetti. "Then I'll have to charge you for what you owe, so you can start watching out. And you, too," he added, looking at Francisco. "Keep your eyes peeled."

The Assistant Justice called the soldier who was assigned to help him enforce the law in Moreira's neighborhood, and he ordered that Moreira be put in the stocks again. Moreira smiled as he let himself be put in the stocks, certain now that he would get his revenge eventually, and he endured the blows and insults without saying a word. He was released the next day and told that this was his last chance to straighten up. Moreira smiled as he heard the final admonition and said only:

"Until next time, then, amigo Francisco."

He spent the rest of the day at home, hugging and kissing his son and Vicenta and playing the most mournful tunes on his guitar. He went to the table at suppertime but couldn't eat. After dark, the gaucho put on clean clothing and slid his silver-handled facón under his tirador at the small of his back. Then he saddled and bridled his dappled bay horse with great care, as if in preparation for a hard day's work. His eyes had an ominous glow.

"Where are you going at this hour?" asked Vicenta, unsettled by his unusual preparations.

"To the house of my compadre Giménez," replied Moreira as he mounted with a leap. "I won't be long."

Vicenta's father, who had come to comfort her when he heard of the renewed troubles, got even less of an answer to the same question.

"I won't be long," said Moreira, who spurred his horse into the night and was gone, his long hair flying in the wind.

The dappled bay raced across the shadowy countryside, responding to the urgency of its rider, who egged the animal on with his voice, impatient to arrive at his destination. After twenty minutes, horse and rider saw the lights of a pulpería, and soon they were right outside. Moreira dismounted and tied his horse to the hitching post with a slip-knot that could be untied in a hurry. Then he stepped inside the pulpería, which was full of gauchos at that hour of the evening.

iv

This was Sardetti's pulpería, and Moreira wanted his ten thousand pesos. In the backroom of the place half a dozen men sat on crates and a rickety chair or two gossiping about the news of our hero's second stint in the stocks. They all stood when they saw Moreira, wishing him well, "God keep you, friend," said one, and several went to squeeze the gaucho's hand. Sardetti went pale, for his guilty conscience clearly announced the purpose of the visit, and he examined the faces of the other customers, trying to discern their loyalties. Moreira seemed self-possessed and defiant. He responded to his well-wishers with a broad smile that shone white in his jet black beard, then turned to Sardetti.

"Serve me a drink, barkeeper," he said, just as calmly as you please and then shouted to the other men. "The next round is on me, boys."

Sardetti hurried to fill the glasses of all his customers, who raised them and drank to the health of Juan Moreira.

"Yes, sir," he said to no one in particular, "if somebody thinks that he can milk this cow without a hobble, well, he might get gored."

Moreira ordered another round for everyone, and continued:

"Patience just runs out, sometimes, like mine has. Who knows where it's run to . . . straight to the devil, I expect. It ran out last night when our friend Francisco put me in the stocks again for nothing. But today the cow has turned into a bull, looks like."

Sardetti listened, gulping. He knew not to expect empty words from Juan Moreira, who continued his soliloquy with quiet firmness.

"All of you know I lent this man ten thousand pesos," he said, pointing at Sardetti with his riding whip. "But he didn't pay me back, so I went to our Assistant Justice, and do you know what? He called me a thief and said I wasn't owed a thing!"

As he pronounced these last words, Moreira's voice trembled, and his eyes teared with rage.

"It's true, friend Moreira," responded Sardetti quickly and with humility. "I just didn't have the money, and I would have lost my business, see? But I know that I owe you, and I'm going to pay you some day."

Moreira continued his soliloquy as if not hearing Sardetti at all, and the other men knew, then, why the gaucho was there, and knew, too, what they were about to witness.

"Then they put me in the stocks like a criminal and beat me," said Moreira, signaling a bruise on his brow, "when I couldn't defend myself, and then turned me out this morning, like a branded steer, threatening to send me to the army."

One of his listeners, an older man and a good friend of Moreira's, interrupted gently to tell him that revenge on a cowardly *gringo* like Sardetti wasn't worth becoming an outlaw.

"You have a young son," concluded the older man, "and the boy will suffer the consequences of your act. Stop now, for your son's sake. Stop, and we'll have one for the road."

An enormous sorrow covered Moreira's handsome face.

"No, friend," he said sadly, "I can't go until I do what I came for. I don't want one for the road, either, thank you. I don't want anybody to say I had to get my courage from a bottle." Standing up suddenly, he turned to the merchant and said, in a different voice: "Sardetti, I've come for my money, or to charge you the penalty for not paying, just as I promised."

"I don't have it now," whined the Italian. "Wait a few more days, and I swear I'll pay every peso."

"My ten thousand pesos, right now," said the gaucho, holding out his palm, "or I'll charge you the penalty I have in mind. No one can say I don't keep *my* word, no matter what the cost."

The customers froze silently in place. The storeowner said nothing. Moreira drew his facón, which glinted dully in the lamplight, and wrapped his poncho of vicuña around his left arm. He had become an avenging angel. He leapt over the counter at Sardetti, and many of the onlookers closed their eyes to avoid watching the mayhem. A silence followed, however. Those who had closed their eyes opened them to find Moreira standing motionless in front of Sardetti. The gaucho had seen that Sardetti was unarmed, and he refused to kill an unarmed man.

"I'm unarmed, you see?" said the Italian. "And even if I weren't, this would still be murder."

Moreira pulled a facón from the belt of someone standing nearby and tossed it at Sardetti's feet. The Italian grabbed the facón, and his expression of terrified resignation and humility vanished. Extending his blade toward Moreira, he waited. The customers and Sardetti's fourteen-year-old clerk, paralyzed with fear, rapidly cleared the back room, illuminated from above by a kerosene lantern, where only Moreira and Sardetti remained, silently taking each other's measure in the dim light.

"That's more like it," muttered the gaucho, observing Sardetti's new attitude, and attacked with full force. Sardetti dodged Moreira's first thrust and delivered one in return, which Moreira caught easily in the poncho on his left arm. For two minutes the two men fought without one being able to wound the other. Sardetti, realizing that time was not on his side, given the younger man's superior stamina, lunged forward to kill or be killed. Even though Moreira raised his poncho and twisted his torso to avoid the thrust, Sardetti's facón penetrated several folds of the poncho and pierced the defender's chest, very slightly, but enough to bloody his shirt. The gaucho looked down at his chest and smiled.

"That's more like it," he shouted, and raising his poncho as a shield, he lowered his head and charged like a bull.

Sardetti gave a dull groan as Moreira's blade went in. The storeowner dropped his weapon with a clatter and stood swaying with a dazed expression.

"One," said Moreira, and then, like lightening, he stabbed the storeowner nine more times, counting aloud, once for each thousand pesos of the bad debt. Sardetti was dead before he hit the floorboards.

The avenging angel looked at the storekeeper's inert body for a moment, glanced at the still-frozen onlookers, and was out the door, saying:

"Now, come what may, I've done what I had to."

He untied his horse, mounted, and rode away unhurriedly, as if he had some thinking to do before he arrived at his destination.

V

His family awaited him at home with deep anxiety. Judging by the train of earlier events and by Moreira's preparations on that fatal evening, Vicenta's father had guessed the gaucho's intentions, and he fully expected to learn that Moreira had settled accounts with all his tormenters that night, beginning with Sardetti, and that anyone who stood in the way was likely to die, too.

"You can't treat a man like Juan in that manner and get away with it," said the old man. "If they push him too hard, they are going to regret it."

His somber comments upset Vicenta even more, and she dissolved in tears. Taking her father's hands in her own, she begged him to go find her husband and bring him home. She, too, suspected the true nature of the evening's errand.

"What Juan went to do not even the devil himself can prevent, I'm afraid," said her father, smiling sadly. "His mind was made up."

"What if they kill him, papá?" inquired Vicenta, beside herself.

"There aren't enough soldiers in Matanzas to kill Juan Moreira," replied her father, and his adamant conviction raised his daughter's battered spirits.

The neighing of Moreira's horse outside, just then, launched the old man out of his chair and wrung a cry of relief from Vicenta. The two went out into the night, and although the gaucho could not yet be seen, they heard the familiar clinking of his spurs as he approached in the darkness. Vicenta ran toward the sound and threw herself into her husband's arms. Moreira comforted Vicenta and extended his hand to his father–in–law, and his strong and lingering handshake silently confirmed what had happened. The old man lowered his head thoughtfully and said nothing. Moreira seemed tranquil, but a storm raged silently behind his eyes. This reporter has talked with many soldiers, including the police chiefs of Navarro and Lobos, now invalids, who had an encounter with Moreira, and all of them speak of the eerie look in Moreira's manly eyes during the fight, his pupils dilated beneath his long lashes, like the gaze of a lion.

The gaucho asked his wife to prepare him a gourd of mate to drink, and no sooner had she gone to do so, than he took her father's hand in both of his own, speaking softly and with infinite melancholy.

"I've killed a man, and you know what that means," he said.

The older man looked up at Moreira tearfully.

"Was it in a fair fight?" he asked.

Moreira said nothing but opened his jacket to reveal the bloody shirt underneath, and the old man nodded.

"What will you do now, Juan?" he asked.

"I'll need to go away for a few days, until it blows over. I killed only Sardetti, because I went by Francisco's house and he wasn't there. He can run, but he can't hide. His turn will come."

The Assistant Justice had gone to the office of the Justice of the Peace in town to report Moreira's second stint in the stocks and tell a pack of lies, just as had occurred on the first occasion.

"Papá," said the gaucho to his father-in-law, "I'll need you to take care of Vicenta and Juancito while I'm away. God knows when I can return, and it isn't right for them to suffer because of me. I'll saddle up before dawn to go by the house of my compadre Giménez on my way out of Matanzas."

Moreira spent the rest of the night conversing with Vicenta, not about what had happened but, rather, about domestic matters and work to be done, for he was determined to spare her a description of the killing, although she could well imagine it, having seen blood on the hilt of his facón and several long slashes in his poncho. At the first light of dawn, Moreira dressed and spent a very long time inspecting his horse's saddle and bridle, adding a number of supplies that he ordinarily carried with him only when he went to fight Indians with the national guard. He also tucked a scatter-shot trabuco into his tirador. He kissed Vicenta and stood for a long time watching Juancito, still peacefully asleep, then he shook his father-in-law's hand, mounted, and set off.

For a quarter of an hour, Moreira rode with bowed head, his chin on his chest, holding the reins only loosely. God only knows how he suffered in that moment. Now his martyrdom had begun in earnest. He knew that, if caught, now the army would be his certain punishment. He had seen it happen to so many other gauchos like himself. He stopped, turned, and stood in his stirrups and looked back toward his little house, a white dot in the horizon, then dropped heavily back into the saddle, as two enormous tears rolled down his cheeks.

The gaucho arrived at the house of his friend Giménez, whom he addressed without dismounting.

"Compadre, last night I killed Sardetti," said Moreira, as his friend approached, "so I have to go, and I'm leaving everything that I have in the world back there at my house."

Both men looked thoughtfully in the direction of Moreira's house.

"I've come to ask that you take care of things for me while I'm gone. Vicenta's father is getting old, and you understand laws and such and can deal with the authorities. Troubles never come singly, as they say. Protect them for me, compadre."

Giménez asked what had happened, and Moreira told him, not omitting any detail, but when Giménez began to lament the awful consequences, Moreira cut him short.

"What's done is done, and there's no use crying. At least Sardetti has gotten what he deserved, and Francisco will get the same. But as for my family, compadre, I'm putting them in your hands." Moreira's tone changed, and he choked up as he concluded, "Take care of them, and you can count on me for the rest of my life."

And without further leave-taking, without so much as a backward glance, Moreira rode away. Giménez stood watching for a moment with arms crossed, as the sun—poncho of the poor, as they say—began to spill over the early morning countryside. Then he saddled the fine animal that Moreira had given him on the occasion of his wedding and trotted to town to learn what measures the Justice of the Peace planned to take against Juan Moreira.

The town of Matanzas was abuzz with the news. Giménez heard the death of Sardetti narrated, more or less favorably, half a dozen times before he tied his horse in front of the office of the Justice of the Peace. The Assistant Justice of Moreira's neighborhood, which is to say, our friend Francisco, was already riding around with four soldiers of the Matanzas police, and the normal string of abuses had begun. The witnesses to the killing had been arrested and some of them put in the stocks. Moreira's house had been ransacked and Vicenta, her child, and her father taken into custody. Someone had to be punished for the storeowner's death, and in the absence of the killer, his wife and child would serve the purpose. Giménez petitioned for their release but was completely ignored. Vicenta and her father surely knew the bandit's whereabouts and must confess it, explained Francisco. In the meantime, everything belonging to Moreira had been "requisitioned and sequestered" to pay for court costs, which, in practice, meant "confiscated and destroyed." What happened was what always happens when the rural police impound a gaucho's property, his cattle are butchered, his horses given away, his crops abandoned.

Who could save our hero's property and loved ones from this travesty of justice? Only Juan Moreira himself, evidently.

vi

What had become of Moreira? He had traveled to the not-so-distant locality of Saladillo, where he had friends. He never doubted that they would shelter him. Hospitality is a kind of religion on the pampa. And what man with a roof over his own head would deny hospitality to a countryman pursued by "the law," when "the law" is the plague that every gaucho suffers?

Moreira's story—his courtship and marriage, Francisco's harassment, Sardetti's shamelessness, and the scene in the pulpería—made a profound impression on his friends.

"And I'm not finished yet," Moreira concluded with an expression of anguish. "My only concern is for my little son and for Vicenta—and for her father, who's old and sick, and who's probably in the stocks right now on my account. I can't stop wondering if they are all right. . . ."

His words trailed off, and he looked at the ground.

For a long time, none of the half dozen men present dared interrupt the silence that followed Moreira's story, which had brought back painful memories for every one of them. All saw in the distraught gaucho a mirror of their own experiences.

Suddenly one of the men present (the others called him Julián) rose and approached Moreira, who sat slumped with his head down. Julián was poorly dressed, a day laborer or hired hand, but his eyes, slightly moistened by our hero's tale of woe, bespoke intelligence, and his aquiline nose, strength of character. Julián placed his hand familiarly on Moreira's shoulder. Moreira raised his head, and the two men looked at each other quietly for a moment, after which, both smiled. A true gaucho doesn't need words to make himself understood by another one. In the eloquent look exchanged by Moreira and Julián, there had been an offer and an acceptance.

"Rest easy, brother," said Julián. "My going is just as if you went yourself. Tomorrow by this time you'll know if your family is all right."

Moreira embraced his new friend, and all went out together to see him off. Julián left in such a hurry that he forgot his bag of tobacco, cigarette papers, and flint lighter, abandoned where he had been drinking mate.

Moreira did not touch the roasted meat that his host put in front of him. Instead, he picked up the guitar and began to play a sad tune, but stopped suddenly and tossed the instrument aside. The other men respected his silence and did not speak even to each other as they passed the mate gourd from hand to hand. One heard only the slight slurping sound as each drinker drained the gourd before passing it to the next man.

Moreira left the thatch-roofed hut to feed his horse and inspect his saddle and bridle and arrange them on the ground, just so, near the tethered animal should he have to make a sudden escape. A gaucho's saddle is covered with sheep fleece, and it makes a good pillow, which is how Moreira used it then. He lay on the ground all night listening, but he couldn't sleep. Instead, images of recent events flooded through his mind, jumbled with nightmare images of his worst fears for the future.

Finally, the first light of dawn crept across the enormous sky of the pampa, and the darkness began to dissipate. One bird saluted the dawning, and then another. The sheep bleated excitedly as someone let them out of the enclosure where they had spent the night. The first moments of the morning in the countryside are pure enchantment, worthy of the Creator of the Universe, but they could hardly lighten the heavy heart of Juan Moreira, who did breathe the fresh air deeply and with satisfaction as he stood up, relieved by the end of the seemingly interminable vigil. The gaucho watered his dappled bay horse, who wiggled his long ears and gave his master's shoulder an appreciative nuzzle and then a solid nudge, as if to affirm his readiness for the upcoming ride.

Inside the thatch-roofed hut, the other men were making a fire and heating water for mate, with which our early rising gauchos must, without fail, begin each and every day. Moreira sat down with the others, who returned immediately to the conversation of the day before, speculating now about when Julián would return. And there they sat all morning. Various of the men got up to do chores but never all at once. As if by prior agreement, one of them always stayed at the side of the distraught fugitive, attempting unsuccessfully to divert his mind from the threat hanging over his family back in Matanzas.

Moreira did not sleep, as the others did, after the midday meal. An eternity, it seemed, before shadows began to lengthen. Moreira's heartbeat quickened with the thought that Julián could arrive, or not, at any moment. Still it was fully dark before the sound of a horse's hooves could finally be heard, approaching at a gallop. Moreira was the first to hear and the first to greet the dismounting rider.

Julián's woeful face, when it could be seen, gave everything away.

"Courage, friend Moreira," he said, "because you win some and you lose some in this life."

"Spit it out, friend Julián," groaned Moreira, "spit it all out no matter how bitter. I have got the guts to hear it straight."

"Wait a moment, now," replied Julián, "because I've got to start at the beginning to get it right."

The men sat around the smoldering fire where the kettle always bubbled with water for mate. The host served Julián, who did not speak, draining the gourd and passing it to another man.

"In Matanzas, *you* are all people talk about, right now, friend Moreira," said Julián. "You, and the squad of mounted police that has been assigned to find and kill you."

"If they can," snarled Moreira. "But no, go on."

"So it wasn't hard to find things out. The law had your father-in-law Gregorio prisoner for a while, along with Vicenta, but they got nothing out of him and eventually let him go. The old man rode out looking for you, it seems, but the horse got spooked and threw him, and they say he may not recover."

As Julián spoke, Moreira sat pale and trembling.

"Your compadre Giménez did his best to get Vicenta released, but they won't do it, saying that you'll come for her eventually, and Francisco is at your house right now with a couple of soldiers, waiting for you."

"They won't have to wait long," said Moreira, springing to his feet. "They're at my house. It wouldn't be courteous."

And with that he was out the door, followed by the others. Julián got a fresh horse, and all the men began to saddle up. It was a moment before Moreira, absorbed in his own preparations, noticed theirs.

"No, no, friends," he said gratefully, "thank you, but I'm going alone. Don't worry, though, you'll see me again. My time hasn't come yet."

And with that, he gave a last pull on the cinch, threw his poncho over his shoulder, and mounted. His dappled bay horse, bored with the inactivity, whinnied with pleasure upon feeling its rider's weight and sprang forward into the night. As the sound of his galloping horse receded, Julián made a decision.

"That Moreira," he said. "I can't let him go alone."

Checking that his tobacco pouch and his facón were both securely tucked into his tirador, he mounted the fresh horse and followed Moreira's trail into the darkness.

vii

As he advanced across the sleeping countryside, Moreira had to hold back his fiery steed, conserving its energy in case he needed to outrun pursuers. Nevertheless, he made good speed all night and all the next morning, not dismounting until midday, when he came to a small grove of hemlocks that gave protection from prying eyes while allowing him to see approaching riders from far away. He was still many hours' ride from his home in Matanzas. He loosened the cinch, took the bit from his horse's mouth so that it could graze freely, then spread his wool poncho on the grass for himself and lay down on it, alternately surveying the horizon and meditating on how quickly everything in his life had changed.

His horse's whinny called him from his reverie. An answering whinny sounded in the distance, and Moreira leapt to his feet, adjusted the cinch and bit, and peered anxiously in the direction that his horse was looking and angling it ears. After a few minutes, he heard the whinny of an approaching horse again, and there, coming into view on the road, almost a mile away, were horse and rider, still little more than a speck. At that distance, a gaucho can identify a horse or cow by its markings and recognize a rider by his posture in the saddle. Therefore, Moreira could see that the rider was Julián, and Julián, that the horse was Moreira's dappled bay. In the minutes before Julián arrived at the hemlock grove, Moreira loosened his horse's cinch and removed its bit again.

When Julián finally arrived, he found Moreira smiling sadly, and as he put his chestnut horse to graze beside the dappled bay, he felt Moreira pat him on the back.

"What are you doing, friend Julián? I told you that I've got to do this by myself."

"But what about a friend in need?" replied Julián. "And anyway, there is something else that I have to tell you. I didn't say it last night, because it's for your ears only."

So saying, he spread his poncho on the grass beside Moreira's, sat down, rolled a cigarette, and finished the narrative that he had begun on the previous evening.

"There is a bitter thing that you have to know, he explained. "Poison is always bitter, though, so a drop more or less, doesn't make too much difference."

Moreira felt he couldn't breathe as he braced himself for a new revelation that, to judge by the other man's warning preamble, promised to be the most painful one yet.

"One of the first things that I did in Matanzas was go to see Vicenta. When I told her not to cry, that everything will work out, because you have many friends, she cried all the more, and she said the following words, which I've been careful to remember exactly: 'Tell my Juan to forget me. If he comes back they'll kill him, as they killed my father, claiming that he fell off his horse. Tell him to run and not look back. Francisco is determined to send him to the army simply because he is my husband. He told me that last night, but he also promised that he'd leave Juan alone if I agreed to go with him to a place that he has in Navarro.'"

Moreira roared an imprecation, leapt up, readied his horse and mounted it, and was off at a gallop, all more or less in the blink of an eye. He shouted back to the startled Julián, who still sat motionless:

"The devil himself couldn't save him now!"

It was about eight o'clock when Moreira stopped and dismounted only a few hundred yards from his house. Inside were five men: the Assistant Justice, two soldiers, and two of Moreira's erstwhile neighbors. In the moment when Moreira, slipping through the shadows, pressed his eye to a crack in the door, the men were talking about him. On the table stood a bottle of gin and two glasses.

"He was a good *criollo*," one of the neighbors was saying. "What he did, you would have done yourself, Francisco, and a good man deserves some consideration. He's suffered enough already."

"No," replied the Assistant Justice. "I'm going to chase him until I catch him, and when I catch him, I'm going to kill him like a dog, but not before he suffers a lot more. I want him to know that I've got Vicenta. He stole her from *me*, you know. And since she didn't want to be my wife, she can be my *comfort*."

The neighbor was about to reply when the words hardened in his mouth, frozen solid by the chill blast of terror that turned all five seated men into icy statues in an instant. The chill came from the door, which had opened with a loud kick to reveal, outlined against the black, the figure of Juan Moreira, his head held high, his eyes full of lightning bolts, his poncho on his left arm, and in his right hand, the dreadful blade.

"Do you want to see how a man kills a dog, Francisco?"

Moreira's voice trembled with repressed rage. The Assistant Justice was a hardened fighter, and Moreira's words galvanized him to action. He brought out his pistol and fired, but the shot went wide.

"See? That's why you need pointers," laughed Moreira, who seemed to become calmer as the waiting finally ended and the fighting began. "You like to kill from a safe distance," he added, after dodging a second bullet.

Moreira moved forward slowly, smiling. His calm unnerved Francisco, who had no more bullets in his double-barreled pistol. The Assistant Justice turned to the two soldiers:

"Kill him! What are you waiting for?"

The soldiers' fear, as well as certain natural sympathies toward Moreira, had combined to keep them motionless. At the shouts of the Assistant Justice, they remembered themselves, drew their sabers, and attacked Moreira. The bloody scene that ensued became neighborhood lore.

Like a crouching tiger, Moreira awaited, his awful blade extended toward the advancing soldiers, who raised their swords together, as if to split him in two. Unfortunately for the soldiers, both swung at the same time, and both blows sank uselessly into the wall as Moreira leapt to the right and, as the soldiers struggled to recover a defensive posture, forward, pushing his facón into one of them to the hilt, just below the ribcage. The skewered gendarme dropped silently to the floor, and Moreira turned his attention to the other, just in time to catch another saber stroke in his poncho. Then in went the hungry facón, this time deftly between the ribs. The second soldier stumbled, with an expression of surprise, and went down right in front of the Assistant Justice.

He and Moreira found each other face-to-face for the final showdown, with only the two neighbors and the two dead soldiers, all four equally motionless, as witnesses. Because of Francisco's sword, however, their arms were still not equal.

"Now we'll see how you handle yourself in a fair fight, friend Francisco," said the gaucho with astonishing cool, adding, with a blood-chilling smile: "And then we'll see the color of your insides."

It was a clash of titans, two strong, brave men who hated each other profoundly, both knowing that one was about to die. The dim room flashed with the hot lightening of their eyes and the cold lightening of their steel. Moreira's calm was greater because he recognized his superior ability and because he had so much less to lose. He calmly and skillfully diverted Francisco's slashes and thrusts with his poncho without counterattacking, only brandishing his facón as if indecisive about just how to kill his attacker. When Francisco threw his most violent blow yet, leaving himself off balance, Moreira managed to entangle the sword in his poncho and, passing his facón to his left hand, he pulled the sword out of his enemy's grip.

The surprised Assistant Justice retreated until he found his back against the wall, crying for help to Moreira's two neighbors, who remained frozen in place, filled with admiration for Moreira.

"Don't get so excited," said the gaucho to the Assistant Justice. "I am not going to kill you just yet. There are a few things you have to hear first, 'friend' Francisco, as I once considered you. You've persecuted me unjustly, reducing me to my present disgrace, you've beaten me when I was defenseless in the stocks, and not content with that, you've tried to kill me in order to take my wife, whose pure heart you'll never sully, I promise, because, Francisco, now you *are* about to die," Moreira smiled broadly, as if relieved at last of the heavy emotional burden, "and not because I'm afraid of you, no, but only because I want to spare Vicenta your nauseating advances in my absence. So get ready because here I come."

His little speech concluded, the gaucho threw Francisco's sword back to him. The Assistant Justice grabbed the weapon avidly, beaming with relief and happiness, and all his energy returned at once. Beside himself, his eyes wide and his mouth, half-open, he did not wait for Moreira's onslaught but, rather, surged forward with a sword thrust so violent that the two remaining onlookers uttered small, woeful exclamations in the belief that the gaucho could not possibly survive it. They were wrong, of course, and suddenly, the duel had ended. Moreira had deflected the sword thrust in a way that left Francisco's chest close and undefended. The opening was all that Moreira needed.

"I've been murdered," cried the Assistant Justice as he fell backward, blood welling from his chest, his sword clattering to the floor.

"You lie," said Moreira. "You died in a fair fight, and I have two witnesses."

Then, looking closely at the dying man's bloody chest, he leaned over and, with an expression of mild distaste, slipped his blade in again, between two ribs and directly into the beating heart of his enemy, which was stilled immediately. With a glance at the two dead soldiers and another at the speechless witnesses, he sheathed his facón and turned to the door, stopping suddenly just as he reached it and stepping back with his hand on his knife again.

Someone else stood outside the doorway, viewing the scene of carnage inside. Moreira relaxed. It was Julián. The gaucho extended his hand to Moreira after wiping away a tear.

"You've got guts, friend Moreira," he said, shaking the other's hand. "Too bad you've got a quarrel with the law, because at this rate we'll end up without police."

The two went to where Moreira had left his horse, and they found Julián's horse there, too.

"I need to ask a final favor," said Moreira.

"Say the word," replied Julián, "and I'll do it, whatever it may be."

"Go see if you can talk to Vicenta," explained Moreira, "because all the police are likely to come looking for me when they hear about the little ruckus tonight. There won't be anyone guarding Vicenta. Tell her what I've done and that she has nothing more to fear from

Francisco. Tell her that I'll watch out for her, wherever my destiny leads me. Tell her that our compadre Giménez will take care of her while I'm gone. And find my dog, Cacique. He's the only one who can accompany me where I'm bound, and he must be with Vicenta, because he isn't anywhere around the house. Ask her to send me Cacique. I'll be waiting at the house of my compadre Giménez."

viii

Julián left immediately, and Moreira, before mounting to ride to his compadre's house, stood for a moment, lost in thought. He had taken his revenge, now, and he was in no hurry to begin the long flight that would take him far from Matanzas and everything he loved. When his mind turned to Vicenta and Juancito, two hot tears ran down his cheeks. No time for that, though.

Giménez wasn't home when Moreira arrived. He'd been gone since the day before and was expected back soon. Moreira took a seat on the gate and waited calmly, pensively, reins in hand. He didn't worry that the mounted police might appear at any moment. He was ready to take on the whole province.

In town, at the office of the Justice of the Peace, the pursuit had already begun. The two witnesses of the night before had reported the death of the Assistant Justice, and the Justice of the Peace himself had ridden straight to the scene of the crime, followed by the captain and eight remaining soldiers of the Matanzas mounted police. If they expected to find Moreira still at the scene, full of bluster and allowing himself to be captured without difficulty, they were sorely disappointed. And in their haste, they had left Vicenta unguarded, just as Moreira predicted.

Julián was able to see her without having to ask anyone's permission. He told her what had happened and, as she dissolved in tears, asked for the dog, urging haste. The police could return at any moment. Vicenta produced the dog, a lapdog facetiously named Cacique, and then buried her face in the bedclothes where Juancito slept, sobbing disconsolately. Julián regarded her for a moment, stirred by the pitiable sight, and then departed like a flash.

Fifteen minutes later, he dismounted at the house of Giménez, who was absorbed in conversation with Moreira. The soul of discretion, Julián affirmed the completion of his mission, gave Moreira the dog, and withdrew. By that time, Moreira had told his compadre everything (nothing that Giménez didn't already know, however) and reiterated his request for protection of Vicenta and Juancito. Especially he begged that everything possible be done to remove his family from the custody of the Justice of the Peace. Then he joined Julián, who waited outside, and the two mounted. Cacique rode happily on the front of Moreira's sheep fleece saddle.

"I have one more favor to ask, compadre," said Moreira at the last minute.

"Ask," replied Giménez, "because you know that I am your true friend."

"Give me your pair of double-barreled pistols. It looks like I'll need more firearms."

Giménez went inside and returned immediately with two beautiful Lefaucheux pistols, which Moreira tucked into his tirador, with thanks and a wave farewell.

Meanwhile, the Matanzas police force was a whirlwind of activity. They had searched the immediate vicinity without finding Moreira and, so, had returned to the scene of the previous night's dramatic events. They had called the town doctor to play the part of coroner, something scarcely necessary, because every wound that Moreira had made was fatal several times over. They called the gravedigger, who brought three simple pine coffins with him. That night they held a wake, and the next morning, a funeral. Then the captain and remaining eight soldiers of the Matanzas police force left in search of Moreira, whom they expected to find not far away, while the Justice of the Peace wrote his official report.

Moreira and Julián had spent the night at a pulpería ten miles or so to the north. Anticipating speedy pursuit by the police, Julián had struggled eloquently, but also fruitlessly, to convince his friend to get out of the district of Matanzas altogether, but Moreira refused to budge.

"I *want* them to catch up with me," he said. "I want them to see who they are up against."

Moreira wanted to establish a fearsome reputation, and the way to do that was not to flee but, rather, to stand and fight his pursuers. Then the police would think twice about giving him trouble.

"So I'll need you to be on your way," he said to Julián, "because I don't want anyone to say that I'm afraid to face them alone, and I don't want you to be outlawed on my account."

"No way am I leaving," insisted Julián, "until you are safely out of Matanzas."

"I know you've got guts, Julián, but I *want* to face the police alone, staying would be no favor to me."

"Then I won't fight, I promise only to watch, no matter what. Then we'll go to a place I know where you'll be safe."

Moreira shook Julián's hand and said no more. He knew that the gaucho would do as he'd promised. The two walked out to where their horses were tied. Swallows flitted over their heads in the early dawn. Moreira inspected his cinch, bridle, and weapons with extreme attention, taking special care to see that the two double-barreled pistols were primed and ready, as the other man watched, smiling with approval. Then they spread their ponchos on the grass and sat down. The customers who arrived at the pulpería were amazed to see Juan Moreira sitting there placidly.

"Get out of here, friend Moreira," they said, "if you don't want to die. One man, even a brave one like you, can't take on the whole Matanzas police force."

"Why, that's the very reason I'm staying," smiled the gaucho. "Now go on inside because the police might run away thinking I've recruited you all to help me. You, too, Julián. I'm counting on what you promised."

Everyone except Moreira went into the pulpería and spent the morning there, expecting the worst. They had high regard for the young police captain of Matanzas, not to mention the eight soldiers he had with him. The storekeeper worried that the police would think he'd been hiding Moreira, but of course he dared not ask him to leave. It was a shame to see a fine man like Moreira killed, they all agreed, for he had done what any honorable gaucho would do. Many of them would have joined him in the fight, were it not for Moreira's strict injunction to stay away. Only Julián did not share the general pessimism, trusting in Moreira's blade, which, in the old expression, "never told a lie."

Outside, Moreira sat calmly on his poncho of vicuña wool beside his dappled bay horse, petting Cacique and periodically scanning the horizon. It seemed impossible that he was waiting to fight eight or ten well-armed men with orders not to take him alive. As the morning passed, men came and went at the pulpería, some of them hoping to locate the police squad and inform Moreira of its whereabouts. After noon, the intense, lazy silence of siesta time in the country settled over the pulpería. Only Moreira remained awake, but finally even he began to feel sleepy. He made sure his weapons were within easy reach, lay facedown with Cacique at his side, and slept as tranquilly as if he were at home, safe and sound, without the slightest danger. It was the first time in three days that he had really slept, and he moved not at all for half an hour.

Suddenly, a rider appeared on the road, and the shrill bark of little Cacique pierced the heavy, mid-afternoon air. As if jolted by an electric shock, Moreira rose from the ground, weapons in hand. The rider, who had galloped hard to bring the news, shouted to Moreira in great excitement.

"They're coming! The captain and eight soldiers."

Moreira smiled and nodded. Sure enough, a cloud of dust indicated the rapid approach of numerous soldiers less than a mile away.

"Save yourself, Moreira," insisted the man who had brought the warning. "There's still time."

"Thank you for the warning, friend," replied the gaucho. "Now go inside and watch from there. It should be a good show, with nine dancers."

Shaking his head as if to say "what a waste," the man went into the pulpería, and Moreira got ready. He put the reins over his horse's head and turned its right side to the oncoming soldiers. Standing on the left side, he leaned against the horse with his arms on the saddle and his chin on his arms and watched the others arrive. He even crossed his feet to clarify that he was going nowhere. The others' remarks about the police captain's courage and ability had piqued his curiosity.

The approaching riders reined in and stopped only a few yards away from Moreira, who did not budge an inch. The soldiers observed him uneasily and glanced away to avoid his steely gaze. The windows and doors of the pulpería filled with the pallid faces of onlookers. Everyone believed in Moreira's skill and courage, but against nine adversaries simultaneously? Julián was the only one among them who did not fully expect to see Moreira killed, and even he had his doubts. Julián forced a smile, but he had a tear in his eye.

The young police captain and his sergeant rode forward a step or two, casting worried glances at the pulpería packed with onlookers, and the captain addressed Moreira with the familiar formula, despite knowing the answer full well:

"Are you Juan Moreira?" he asked.

"At your service," said Moreira, standing proudly erect and politely touching the brim of his hat, while staying behind the body of his horse.

"Then give yourself up immediately and make no resistance," concluded the captain, putting his hand instinctively on the hilt of his saber.

"Who orders it?" said Moreira in a different, more menacing voice.

"The Justice of the Peace of Matanzas and the captain of police, in the name of the law," concluded the younger man, drawing his sword, in which he was imitated by the sergeant at his side.

Moreira looked for a moment at the unfortunate young man whom destiny had put in his path.

"Turn around, snotnose. Who sent *you* to arrest Juan Moreira? Go home and grow up, and then, if you still want to. . . ."

"You're under arrest!" shouted the brave young captain, digging in his spurs and advancing toward Moreira. "Submit or I shall have to kill you in fulfillment of my orders!"

"Come kill me, then," said the gaucho, drawing the pistols that his compadre had given him and cocking all four barrels.

What happened next happened fast. It was over in much less time than it will take to read about it. The captain and sergeant both charged Moreira, who still stood protected behind the dappled bay, the captain in the lead, with his saber up, and then after two simultaneous shots, flipped back onto his horse's rump, dead, his horse bolting, the captain's body slipping to the ground a few paces away, the sergeant shouting, "Don't let him get away!" And then two more shots, and he went down, as well, in a shower of smoke and sparks.

The other seven soldiers had come around Moreira's horse by this time and, although clearly disconcerted by the deaths of both their officers, charged the gaucho all together. Dropping his pistols, he ducked under the belly of his horse, putting it once again between him and his attackers, who thundered past, unable to get at him. Drawing his facón he slid like quicksilver toward the head of the dappled bay and ducked under its neck just as the last soldier rode past on the other side. Moreira's facón went all the way through the soldier's body before the unfortunate man knew what had happened. He, too, slipped off his horse, landing beside the sergeant with a scream of "God help me!"

Demoralized, the remaining six soldiers backed away from Moreira, who still stood where he had begun the fight, beside the dappled bay. Deciding that discretion was the better part of valor, they wheeled and galloped off. Moreira jumped on his horse and waved his facón at the retreating soldiers.

"Cowards!" he shouted happily. "They take a few hits, and they run off like a bunch of ostriches."[1]

He smiled as Cacique, who had disappeared for a few minutes, emerged from somewhere to celebrate his master's triumph. Moreira looked at the three fallen policemen. Only the sergeant was still alive, breathing with difficulty and tightly holding a bloody bullet wound in his side. Moreira sheathed his facón, dismounted, and, holding his reins the whole time, carefully examined the man's wound.

"It's nothing, pal," he concluded. "I've seen men survive worse."

Approaching the counter of the pulpería, he ordered a glass of cane liquor from the storekeeper, who served it somewhat mechanically, being still, like the other onlookers, lost in astonishment at the scene he had just witnessed. Moreira went back to the wounded sergeant, knelt, and gave him a drink of the liquor. Then, untying the man's kerchief from around his neck, Moreira soaked it in liquor as an antiseptic and put it on the wound as a bandage.

"They'll take you to town and remove the bullet. Let nobody say that Juan Moreira is cruel to those he has defeated."

Then, leading his dappled bay by the reins, Moreira went back to the pulpería, where Julián still stood motionless. Over and over, he had thought that his friend could not survive the fight, and the supreme effort by which he had resisted going to Moreira's aid had left him rigid. Moreira held out his hand, and Julián gave him an *abrazo* so powerful that it seemed they might be permanently stuck together.

"Thank you, friend Julián," said the gaucho. "See? It doesn't take more than one real man to scatter a bunch of cowards like that, and they're *all* like that."

Moreira spoke with conviction. He trusted that he could take on the police of the whole province of Buenos Aires with the same serenity and the same outcome.

"God keep you, Moreira," responded Julián. "You are the bravest man that I've ever met, but now every lawman in the province is going to be after you."

"And I'll fight every one of them," affirmed Moreira fiercely. "What do I have to lose? I don't have anything left in the world except what I'm wearing. My sheep and carts are gone, and I don't expect that I'll ever see my family again. So I might as well fight these

1. Actually Moreira is referring to the *ñandú*, or rhea, the smaller South American relative of the ostrich, colloquially referred to as the *avestruz*.

cowards until the day when they finally kill me, and that will be a happy day for me, because then my suffering will end."

As he concluded, the gaucho raised a corner of his poncho to wipe away the tears that rolled down his trembling cheeks, giving his manly face an expression of infinite tenderness. The man who never flinched in the face of death, who defeated nine attackers without breaking a sweat, nearly sobbed at the remembrance of his defenseless wife and son. Moreira's actions, no matter how violent, never responded to mean or petty motivations. Now, however, that the meanness of others had made him into an outlaw, he embraced his destiny with all the force of his ardent spirit. Gradually, now, noble impulses began to disappear from his heart of bronze, and little by little it would become filled with hate.

The gaucho dispelled his melancholy with a shake of his magnificent black shoulder-length mane, smiled at the men who had approached him little by little and pressed around him now, and shook Julián's hand for the last time.

"Farewell, my friends," he said. "I'm off to wherever the wind blows me. Who knows when you'll see me again, but whenever it is, I'll buy the drinks."

Putting his little dog on the front of his saddle, he leapt onto his horse and set off at a slow trot. His last words were for the wounded sergeant:

"God keep you, friend. If you pull through, the next time you see me, we'll shake hands."

After some minutes, he wheeled his horse and waved. Then he disappeared around a bend in the road. With the pulpería out of sight behind him, he let go of the reins so that the dappled bay could take whatever direction it chose.

ix

The little dog Cacique became the sole companion of Moreira's wandering life. Gauchos have a special regard for dogs, who serve them in various ways. Sheepdogs do a more effective job at caring for flocks than the best hired hand. They watch over the flocks tire-lessly, managing them with astounding ability, keeping them from straying too far by day, bringing them to the corral to sleep at night. The powerful dogs called *mastines* have a different job. They are large enough to help round up cattle and fierce enough to help protect the gaucho's home and family, keeping any unexpected visitor mounted until called off. In a fight, they are the gaucho's effective allies, able to pull an enemy off his horse. Wild packs of such dogs create a nuisance when they become hungry enough to prey on the flocks of sheep or even, occasionally, herds of cattle. It is common enough to see three or four enormous mastines bring down a steer and tear it to pieces.

Little dogs like Cacique with their shrill barking alert gauchos to lurking dangers. They have a reputation for intelligence and loyalty, their senses are unbelievably acute. Other dogs seem to recognize their sharper sight, smell, and hearing, because when one of these tiny sen-tinels sounds the alarm, the larger dogs charge off immediately in the direction indicated. When these little dogs see their masters in trouble they become almost laughably fierce, and when their masters die, it is not uncommon to see them guarding the grave for a long time. An example could be seen recently in the North Cemetery of the city of Buenos Aires. Some might laugh at the impotent fury of these little guardians, capable at most of ripping the cuff of one's trousers, but more thoughtful people recognize in them a loyalty superior to what one finds in many human beings.

Moreira had need of such a loyal ally. Cacique rode on the front of his saddle, or sometimes behind him, ever vigilant, ever cheerful, wagging his tail at the slightest gesture of his master, who frequently reached back without looking to scratch his bright little head.

The wanderer never slept at night, realizing that sleep was his great-est vulnerability. He slept only at siesta time, in open country, during the sultry hours of early afternoon, when one practically never finds anyone out and about in the heat of the blazing sun. At such times, the gaucho extended his poncho of vicuña wool on the grass beside his horse and lay face down, resting his head on his crossed arms, his reins around his wrist, his weapons underneath his hands, and Cacique curled up by his side. Should the little dog sound the alarm, the sleeping man would be ready to flee or fight at a moment's notice. Occasionally, the little animal got up and patrolled the surroundings, but he never went far and always returned quickly.

Cacique was acutely sensitive to Moreira's moods. In the periods when bitter recollections overcame his master, who sometimes sat and hung his head for hours, the little dog sat up on his hind legs and watched until, finally, heaving an enormous sigh, Moreira looked up. Then Cacique scampered into the man's lap and licked his hands, as if intentionally distracting him from his sorrow.

When Moreira stopped at a pulpería for a meal, he found fodder for his horse and then roasted a piece of meat to share with Cacique. He always found a warm reception from the other customers, whether in solidarity, because he was recognized, or simply because his manly good looks captivated anyone who met him. He never spent the night at a pulpería, however, and never set foot in a town except when absolutely necessary.

Moreira's life depended on the speed and stamina of his dappled bay horse, which the gaucho literally never unsaddled. Instead, he was careful not to tighten the animal's cinch overmuch, except in emergencies, and he carried a piece of oil cloth to keep the fleece-covered saddle dry in case of rain. He never rode very far without giving the animal a chance to rest, and normally never rode faster than a trot to conserve his horse's strength for a moment of unexpected need. The men at pulperías sometimes arranged impromptu horse races, contests that the dappled bay always won. This superb stallion had been given him as a token of esteem by a fine gentleman, Doctor Adolfo Alsina, about whom the reader is shortly to learn.

X

One day, Moreira rode into the district of Navarro, looking for refuge, because of the good reputation he'd established there years ago. Back then, the Justice of the Peace in Navarro was a young gentleman named José Correa Morales who had asked Moreira to be his police sergeant. Moreira had accepted because the Morales family had been good to him. Imagine Moreira as a lawman!

He had been a dashing and efficacious sergeant when riding around the town and the surrounding pampa with his small squad of mounted police, and no criminal could resist his arrest. Everyone was on his best behavior when Sergeant Juan Moreira was around. When word reached town of some defiant rural bandit, though, Moreira rode out alone to get him. He always began by talking to the man, trying to convince him that resistance was useless and, if that didn't work, capturing him in a fight, one-on-one, a procedure that gave him great prestige among country and townspeople alike. Its renowned police sergeant made Navarro into one of the most law-abiding counties in all Buenos Aires Province. When José Correa Morales stepped down as Navarro's Justice of the Peace, his successor tried to convince the famous gaucho to stay on as police sergeant, but Moreira refused.

"I'm tired of being the law," he explained. "I'd rather go back to Matanzas, look after my cattle, and maybe get married."

Moreira returned to Matanzas, where, as the reader knows, a travesty of justice forced him down the slippery slope of crime. Now he was back in Navarro, where everyone had heard about the events that turned him into an outlaw, including his killing of an Assistant Justice, but still they welcomed Moreira back, such a mighty reputation had he made for himself during his time as police sergeant.

In Navarro, as throughout the small towns and rural areas of the Province of Buenos Aires, emotions ran high around the deeply divisive upcoming election. The two parties that disputed control of the provincial government were vigorously recruiting adherents to join the electoral associations that political parties form on such occasions. Election day was only two months away when Moreira reappeared, preceded by his formidable fame, and he was immediately surrounded by representatives of both parties, each seeking to enlist him in its ranks. The gaucho resisted all the seductive proposals made to him, however. He proudly refused even the offer to arrange for all charges against him in Matanzas to be dropped so that he could go back home in peace after ensuring electoral triumph for the party that made him the offer.

At that point, recalling Moreira's personal loyalty to Doctor Adolfo Alsina, the distinguished citizen whom the gaucho had served as a trusted bodyguard during some very dangerous times, leaders of Alsina's party got him to write to Moreira, asking him personally to join. When Moreira received the letter, he could not deny his friend's request to lend his powerful prestige to the worthy cause.

In his new role as electoral *caudillo*, or political boss, Moreira immediately began to attract voters away from the opposing party. He was more beloved and more feared than the Justice of the Peace, at the time an extremely correct and honorable gentleman named Carlos Casanova. As for the ten or so members of Navarro's local mounted police, some of whom had served under Moreira during his time as sergeant, they trembled at the thought of being sent to arrest him.

The elections approached and two parties, armed to the teeth, readied themselves to determine the outcome *by reason or by force*, to quote the motto that unfortunately still prevails in this supposedly civilized nation.

The opposing side boasted its own caudillo, another gaucho of tremendous personal prestige on the pampa of Navarro. Leguizamón, for that was the man's name, was a tough gaucho, valiant to an extreme, who had a multitude of personal adherents among the countrymen of that locality. He and Moreira were destined for a showdown on election day, and the leaders of Leguizamón's party made sure to prick their champion's pride by praising the deeds of the opponent. Leguizamón was tall and thin, but taut and powerful, and about forty-five years old, considerably older than Moreira. He had fought many knife duels in the pulperías, where gauchos gathered to drink and carouse on the pampa of Buenos Aires, and his fearsome reputation was well deserved.

The trial of strength between Moreira and Leguizamón promised to be spectacular. Leguizamón was reputed the more skillful fighter, but Moreira's cleverness and coolness under pressure, his agility and the power of his attack, compensated for the older man's experience. Leguizamón had the eye of a lynx, his knife arm moved like greased lightning, and his lean frame had the suppleness of a reed, allowing him to dodge the best aimed thrust of his attackers. The people of Navarro had told Moreira all this, to which he had replied with calm resolve:

"We'll see."

Likewise, they had told Leguizamón about Moreira's exploits and received a different sort of answer:

"I won't even break a sweat when I kill that coward. When he gets in my way I'm going to skewer him on my knife the way you skewer a rack of lamb to roast it on a spit."

The contest between these two fighters engrossed the attention of the men of Navarro so thoroughly that they planned to go to town on election day less to vote than to witness the fight between Leguizamón and Moreira. Men talked of little else, each man predicting the representative of his own party would emerge the winner.

Election day finally arrived, and a surprisingly large crowd gathered at the polling place in front of the town church. The arguments surrounding the fight had by that time become so heated that more than one knife fight had already occurred between partisans of Leguizamón and supporters of Moreira.

Moreira took his place among those of his party, wearing his finest clothes. He had used the money that always flows freely at election time to deck out his dappled bay horse with silver-trimmed bridle and saddle gear. The tirador that encircled his waist was encrusted, in classic gaucho style, with gold and silver coins. Thrust under his belt at his belly and sides were two magnificent trabucos of gleaming bronze (a gift from his party) and the two pistols given him by his compadre Giménez on the day that he left Matanzas. Also under his belt, worn diagonally across the small of his back, was the sheath of his long facón, its two-foot-long blade well baptized in blood, as we have seen, its heavy silver handle inlaid with gold within easy reach of his powerful right hand. He carried his poncho of vicuña wool on his left arm and with that hand held the reins of his horse and, from time to time, made the animal do a few showy steps, which it did gladly, with evident pride in its rider and pleasure in responding to him.

Moreira, as calm as could be, made soft, soothing sounds to his horse, smiled at his friends, and occasionally turned to glance at his little dog, Cacique, who rode behind the saddle wagging his tail and looking around him with an inquisitive expression.

On the other side of the table with its poll watchers and ballot box, amid the ranks of the opposing party, was Leguizamón, glowering menacingly in Moreira's direction. Occasionally he stroked his beard with a right hand, a silver-handled whip hanging from his wrist.

Moreira paid him no attention and avoided eye contact. The men on both sides of the table, including those in charge of the polling, were pale with excitement. The electoral officials pretended to inspect their lists of registered voters while watching Moreira and Leguizamón out of the corners of their eyes for signs of the mortal combat that they expected to begin at any moment.

The voting finally began. One by one the voters rode up to the table, dismounted, identified themselves, deposited their printed ballots in the ballot box, got back on their horses, and returned to the group to which they belonged.

After only half an hour or so, Leguizamón spurred his horse forward and, without dismounting, struck the table with his whip. Moreira's party was committing fraud, he said, and he refused to tolerate it. As he spoke, the menacing caudillo glared, not at the electoral officials to whom he ostensibly directed his words, but at Juan Moreira, who ignored the words and declined to respond to the provocation. No one dared to say anything to Leguizamón, who spoke again with increasing insolence.

"You heard me. They're cheating us, and they brought this man along to help them," he said, pointing at Moreira with his whip.

Moreira did not twitch an eyebrow, and he replied to the furious gaucho with apparent tranquility and good humor.

"Don't act like such a jackass, friend. Straighten up and try to show a little more respect, why don't you?"

The men in charge of the polling place held their breath without so much as smiling, while Leguizamón went livid.

"Shut your mouth and get off your horse!" he shouted, dismounting. "You think that you can scare everybody with your looks. Come on, now, put up or shut up!"

At Leguizamón's waist was a revolver and a facón as long as Moreira's, which he brandished as he shouted. Moreira reluctantly slid off his cream-colored horse, drew his own facón, and twirled his poncho of vicuña wool around his left arm to serve as a shield. He had hardly stepped away from his mount when the other man was upon him.

The knife duel between these two gauchos was awesome to behold. Each thrust, each slashing attack would have killed a lesser man instantly, yet the fighters stopped, or dodged, or parried each with astounding skill. The flashing blades soon made tatters of the ponchos which both gauchos had wrapped around their left arms. Yet not a drop of blood had been spilled. Leguizamón grew more blindly enraged with each passing minute and began to make clumsy mistakes. The spectators had opened a wide circle around the fighters, and no one thought of trying to separate them, which would have been foolish and possibly fatal. The older man was slowing, becoming visibly fatigued, while Moreira, not only younger but astutely economizing his strength, seemed acute and agile and ever more able to anticipate his antagonist's lunging assaults.

After fifteen minutes, it seemed that the duel could not last another minute. Someone was bound to drop his guard, to trip, something. Leguizamón began to give ground, his clothing hanging in shreds. Moreira's poncho was completely gone. He stopped the other's knife blows with what remained of his hat. Back, back, back went Leguizamón, until his retreat was stopped by the long table that the electoral officials had long since abandoned, and, pressed against it, he reached for his revolver with his left hand, leaving himself open.

And it was over.

Moreira made a feint toward the other man's belly, and when Leguizamón lowered his blade to parry that thrust, Moreira lunged forward and pounded the hilt of his facón into his faltering opponent's forehead, dropping him unconscious into the dirt without a murmur.

What everyone expected next was for the victor to slice the defeated man's throat from ear to ear, but Moreira didn't do that. Instead, he wiped the copious sweat that had pasted his long hair to his forehead, took two steps back, and still panting, turned to the men of Leguizamón's party that stood looking at him in astonishment.

"Take him somewhere to sleep it off," he said. "And keep him away from here."

"Bravo!" shouted the men of both parties spontaneously. An immense applause greeted Moreira's generous action. He had defeated a valiant and formidable opponent and spared the man's life when it was his customary right to take it.

Instead, he sheathed his facón, mounted his horse, and announced to the assemblage:

"Let the election proceed, gentlemen."

He returned to his place in the ranks of his party, and the voting recommenced in orderly fashion. What happened next may surprise some readers, but it is the normal thing for rural elections in which men cast their ballots for one candidate or another out of deference to a powerful patron, be he a large landowner or the local Justice of the Peace. Moreira's behavior had made such a strong impression on the gauchos of the opposing side that, motivated not by fear but by respect, all of them who had yet to deposit their ballots opted to vote for Moreira's candidate, who won easily as a result.

Leguizamón was carried to Olazo's store, which still exists in Navarro, and where he got some first aid and eventually recovered consciousness. When he realized what had happened, that Moreira had found him somehow not worth killing, he immediately wanted to return to the polling place and renew his challenge, but four or five men held him back. Olazo's store is only three blocks from the town square where the election was being held, and a steady stream of men came by discussing the triumph of Moreira's party, his skill in knocking out Leguizamón, and his fine gesture in sparing the fallen caudillo's life.

Leguizamón's ire increased steadily, and he began shouting at each group of men who brought news from the polling place.

"That coward took advantage of me, seeing me lose my footing because of the table. If not, he'd be dead right now, and I'm still going kill him. Just you wait!"

The men around Leguizamón tried to take him to his house, but he wouldn't go. He ordered a drink and declared that he was going to wait for Moreira right there and kill him to show everybody that the gaucho was all bluff.

When the voting concluded and the crowd began to scatter, the majority of the men headed for their favorite watering hole, Olazo's store. They were not surprised to find Leguizamón there, because they assumed that he would not be content to let the matter stand. They knew that the fight wasn't over.

Moreira had stayed behind for a few minutes, conversing with the electoral officials, who recommended that he avoid Leguizamón and that, were that not possible, Moreira should simply ignore the older man's provocations because he was always drunk and didn't know what he was saying. Moreira understood that the advice was given for his own good, that despite the outcome of the fight, people weren't so sure that he would survive a rematch with Leguizamón, who still had conserved his deadly reputation. Therefore, he smiled, thanked them for their advice, and turned his cream–colored horse toward Olazo's store, very much on purpose.

It was about five o'clock when he turned the corner near the store, which was thronged at that hour. An electric shock energized the men gathered there. Noticing the sudden excitement in their voices and the looks they gave one another, Leguizamón knew that his enemy was coming. Draining the glass in his hand, he stepped out into the street. The blade of the facón in his right hand flashed in the evening sun.

Moreira ignored him and continued to advance at a slow, jingling trot. Leguizamón swore at him copiously, but Moreira's tranquil demeanor and smiling face remained unaltered. Finally, when the rider had approached within two yards of Leguizamón, the enraged gaucho lunged toward him and grabbed the reins of his horse. Quickly but without the slightest sign of agitation, Moreira slid off his mount, drew his awesome facón, and prepared to fight.

Leguizamón attacked with such berserk fury that for four or five minutes he kept Moreira on the defensive, parrying a series of blows so violent that all the defender's alertness and strength were required to avoid being stabbed through or slashed open. The wide-eyed crowd held its breath and watched in tremulous silence. The police knew well enough what was happening but had declined to approach the scene of the encounter, much less intervene in it.

Leguizamón eventually became winded and paused to catch his breath, at which Moreira instantly took the offensive. Our protagonist had not retreated one step during his adversary's concerted attack. Now he moved forward like a hurricane, and his adversary had no choice but to give ground, at first step by step, then in a series of leaps, the only way to avoid Moreira's whirling facón. Leguizamón retreated for the entire three blocks between Olazo's store and the town square and, in that way, avoided being wounded. No blood had been drawn all day except for a slight wound on Moreira's left arm.

The onlookers followed them down the street, those who had been at the store gradually joined by a multitude of men and boys who came running as word of the fight spread through Navarro. The town's squad of mounted police stood in front of the Justice of the Peace's office holding their horses' bridles. All they did was watch as Moreira backed Leguizamón against the front of the church where the election had recently taken place. Raising his left arm to ward off Leguizamón's last-gasp counterattack, Moreira dove forward at full length with his facón stretched out before him, burying it to the hilt in Leguizamón, who bellowed for the last time as his life left his body, which fell with a dull thud onto the steps of the atrium.

Moreira left his facón in the fallen body and, turning to the multitude of spectators, he crossed his arms and looked at them for a moment before addressing them.

"If anyone wants to challenge what I've done, say it now," he told them.

Nobody moved or said a word. The gauchos' silence signaled approbation of Moreira's actions.

Moreira looked down, leaned over, and pulled his knife from the still-quivering body of Leguizamón. The wound gushed blood, and the quivering stopped. Moreira gazed at the body in silence for a moment, as if regretful, and then, leaving the knife on the corpse, mounted his horse with a somber expression, gently controlling Cacique, who licked Moreira's hands, then attempted to lick his face in celebration. Riding over to the office of the Justice of the Peace, Moreira addressed the trembling sergeant of the guard.

"Excuse me, friend. I forgot my knife," he said, and pointed to the bloody knife that he had left on Leguizamón's chest. "Could you hand it to me?"

Obediently, the sergeant gave the reins of his horse to one of the soldiers, went and got Moreira's knife, and surrendered it to him without a murmur. Moreira put the knife in its sheath after wiping it on his horse's mane. Then he wheeled and, with a kick of his spurs, trotted away, leaving his astonished audience openmouthed.

This is fact, not fiction. The events narrated here can be confirmed by Correa Morales or by Casanova, who was Justice of the Peace at the time, and by many other witnesses to what I've described. There are episodes in the life of Juan Moreira that exceed anything a novelist could imagine. Other famous bandits cannot compare to him. A lot has been made of men like Luigi Vampa and Diego Corrientes whom the local police never had any problem arresting, whereas Juan Moreira single-handedly defeated the soldiers sent to capture him on repeated occasions.

Let us return to our story.

xi

After the fight with Leguizamón, Moreira remained in the district of Navarro for considerable time. His greatest diversions were the dances and other gatherings held at local pulperías. Moreira customarily drank his fill at these events, without the occurrence of any trouble whatsoever. Whereas drink makes many men testy and belligerent, just the opposite happened with our hero. Alcohol made him gentle and good humored. He liked to invite other men to play at knife-fighting, just for fun, using sticks instead of knives. He seldom got any takers, naturally, which made him laugh and look around for any half-tamed horses on which he might exercise his abilities as a horse tamer. Even after several drinks, he could ride a bucking horse without being thrown until it accepted him. In the same state, Moreira was a crack shot with a pistol, shattering any bottle placed in front of him at forty paces.

At other times, though, the old melancholy settled over him. If the pulpería had rooms to rent, Moreira shut himself inside one of them, and outside the door one could hear him sobbing for hours. No one dared disturb him then, and he did not emerge until he had given full vent to his grief, at least for a while. When he left the room, the gaucho went first to find his dog and to make sure that his horse had food and water. They were all the family he had left and represented all that he had ever loved. Cacique had been a gift from Vicenta, and the dappled bay, from Adolfo Alsina, as the reader already knows.

Let us consider the situation in which the gaucho received this splendid gift, for it will show us another side of Moreira's life in the years before he became an outlaw.

During the 1860s, the politics of Argentina went through troubled times. Some of our most distinguished leaders, men such as Bartolomé Mitre and many others, found themselves threatened with assassination. Doctor Alsina, a doctor of law, was one of those under threat, and his party found him the best bodyguard possible, a fine-looking young gaucho from the district of Matanzas whose reputation for bravery was already well established, our hero Juan Moreira.

Moreira took a great liking to Alsina, whose shadow he became for a long time, and the doctor of law, being an excellent judge of character, liked Moreira as well. Alsina treated the young gaucho not as a hired thug, but as a comrade who had come to share in hardships and dangers. Alsina knew how to talk to a gaucho, using simple, honest, straightforward language. Simplicity and honesty go straight to a gaucho's heart and make of him a friend. Our gauchos make a sort of religion out of friendship, and nothing could be simpler than to befriend one. All it takes is understanding his simple, virtuous heart and speaking to him with dignity and affection, a sort of treatment that gauchos are not accustomed to receive from city folk. When a social superior treats him as an equal, man to man, the gaucho feels an immediate fondness toward the man, whom he is apt to term a good criollo, and soon considers a friend for life. And once your friend, the gaucho becomes as docile as a child whom you can direct with a look of your eye.

That is exactly the way things went with Alsina and Moreira. Gaucho and politician became inseparable, by day Moreira never left Alsina's side, stuck to him like the echo of his footstep, as they say, and at bedtime the gaucho spread his poncho in the patio and lay there to guard the door of Alsina's bedroom all night.

When the political situation finally normalized and the danger passed, Moreira's services were no longer needed, and so the gaucho naturally wanted to return home from Buenos Aires and take care of the livestock that his neighbors had been watching during his long absence. Doctor Alsina did not want to let him go and made a series of generous offers designed to try to keep Moreira at his side, to no avail. The gaucho felt suffocated in the great city and needed to return to the pampa, the place for which he was best suited by habit and temperament. So Alsina gave up trying to keep Moreira in the city, bought him a train ticket, and bid him farewell with a large cash bonus in recognition of his services.

The gaucho blanched when he saw the money, and one of those big tears rolled down his cheek into his still-incipient beard. Doctor Alsina quickly realized his blunder and withdrew the handful of cash, as Moreira explained his reaction:

"To pay me would be an insult that I don't deserve, boss. I have guarded you out of friendship."

Profoundly moved by the nobility of the gaucho's sentiments, Alsina first offered his hand and then, a hearty abrazo. The gaucho's resentment abated instantly, so proud was he to receive an abrazo from a university-educated gentleman. Holding his head high, he stepped back after a moment, with evident emotion:

"If you ever need me to protect you again, sir, only say the word, and I'll come right away, although it be from the end of the earth. From this day forward, I am your man."

Moreira left speedily, and Alsina stood meditating on the nobility of our gauchos and on their cruel fate—to be deprived of their rights and systematically abused by their social betters, who think that these remarkable countrymen of ours are worthless beings, fit only to be deployed as hired thugs at election time or conscripted into the army and sent to the frontier. The proper response to a gaucho's friendship is not payment, but friendship in return, which may be expressed in the kind of gift one man gives another.

So Alsina bought the most magnificent horse to be found in all Buenos Aires, a beautiful dappled bay stallion, and sent it to Moreira along with another gift, a long facón, its silver handle inlaid with gold. And that is how the gaucho came by these valuable possessions and why they meant so much to him, apart from their inherent value and usefulness.

Let us return to the second period of Moreira's life in the district of Navarro, where he was again to play a similar role. After the election that we witnessed, the violent clashes between political parties continued. A certain gentleman by the name of Marañón represented a powerful faction of the party that Moreira supported, and for that reason, Marañón became the target of assassination attempts. The enemies who hired the assassins were gentlemen whose names I will omit because of the high political positions that they occupy today. After several failures, they hired five gauchos with tough reputations and gave them forty thousand pesos to eliminate Marañón once and for all.

A large moon floated in the clear sky over the town of Navarro on the night that the victim was scheduled to die. Marañón knew that his life was in danger, but having a courageous heart, he went out that

evening, as he always did, to the Navarro social club, accompanied
only by the revolver that he carried in his pocket. He stayed at the
club until eleven o'clock, playing a quiet game of billiards with various acquaintances. Then he walked home alone through the moonlit
streets, taking a shortcut through a hemlock grove where, as luck
would have it, the five murderers awaited with knives drawn. The
young gentleman strode along fearlessly, and he had gone no more
than two or three steps into the trees when the five emerged to cut
him off, knives in hand.

"You can kiss it all good-bye, now," said one of them, as they
advanced toward their victim.

Marañón cocked his revolver and glanced behind him, where he
saw the most disheartening sight imaginable: another man advancing
toward him from behind, a man whom he recognized, in the bright
moonlight, to be none other than Juan Moreira, the same Moreira
who had liquidated Leguizamón in front of half the town of Navarro,
his famous facón glinting in the pallid rays of the moon.

In the next instant, Moreira was on him like a panther, and sliding his arm around the young gentleman's waist, threw him to the
ground the way that gauchos do with a calf at branding time. From
the ground, the half-stunned Marañón watched as the gaucho flew
over him, effortlessly sliced open the belly of the first assailant, and
shouted at the oncoming four:

"Are you ready for Juan Moreira, cowards?"

They definitely weren't, and bolted away silently, in panic, as soon
as they heard the name. Moreira laughed and turned to the young
gentleman who was wobbling to his feet in astonishment.

"Thank you," said the young man, extending his hand. "I'm very
lucky that you happened by."

"I heard they were going to kill you," said the gaucho, "so I
thought I'd just tag along and make sure they didn't."

Then he casually inspected the dead man to make sure he was
dead and went to find the dappled bay, standing in the shadows not
far away.

"I'll escort you home," he said, leading the animal by the reins,
"though I doubt you've much to fear from those cowards. They're
probably still running."

He laughed again, and the two walked without conversing through
the silent, moonlit streets to the gentleman's house not far away.
Marañón was having a hard time absorbing what had just happened.
A man whom he recognized, but had never met, had just saved his

life. In fact, that isn't rare among gauchos. They just "take a shine" to someone, as they say, because of the way he looks, or because of something that they've seen him do. When a gaucho likes you, he does it with the same vehemence with which he loves or hates or gambles or drinks. He likes you, and that's it, and he'll save your life, even at the cost of his own, without thinking twice about it.

When they entered his house, Marañón finally broke the silence.

"Friend Moreira," said the gentlemen, when the two had taken seats inside, "how can I repay you? If there is ever any way, let me know."

"Don't thank me, sir," protested the gaucho. "Anyone would have done the same. I've taken a shine to you, is all. You've got to like somebody in this world. It kind of makes you breathe easier."

And he explained that he had lost everything that he ever cared about and become a wandering pariah.

"But why don't you leave that life and stop provoking them to pursue you?" asked the young doctor of law. "You could settle down and go back to the sort of work that you did before."

Moreira raised his tearful eyes at the kind gentlemen, and his voice cracked a bit as he narrated the details of his sad story, giving the full picture of his conflict with the provincial authorities. Marañón put his hand on the gauchos shoulder as he replied:

"You'll have to leave Buenos Aires Province, then. I could arrange work for you in different province, Córdoba, say, or Santa Fe, where you could settle down and be happy again. I can give you letters of introduction for friends that I have in those provinces. Then, when enough years have passed and everything has been forgotten, you can come back."

"No, I can't go so far from my wife and child," said Moreira, "because if the law can't find me, it will make them suffer for my sake."

"Then I'll see that they go with you, far away," insisted the gentleman, "where you can live peacefully together, and never return to Buenos Aires at all."

But the gaucho was adamant.

"I see that you are a true friend," he said, "and believe me, I appreciate your good intentions, but I can't accept any proposal like that until I find out what has happened to them. They may not even still be alive, and payback time may not be over yet."

Marañón tried to persuade Moreira for a few more minutes but eventually gave up. The gaucho respectfully took his leave, mounted, and disappeared in the night, with his head hanging forward on his chest and the reins abandoned on his horse's neck, seeming to doze, lost in bitter meditation, as the dappled bay walked confidently out of town and into the open countryside. Gradually dawn filtered into the moonlight and took it over. Moreira took off his broad-brimmed hat to let the fresh breeze ripple through his hair, and he breathed deeply of the morning air, perfumed with the scent of wild flowers. Taking his bearings, he turned in the direction of the López pulpería, where he often stopped to feed his horse and dog.

He arrived at the pulpería at a fateful moment. As he asked the store-keeper for a bit of corn for the dappled bay, he heard a dispute devel-oping among the gauchos who were gathered at the pulpería for an "eye-opener." A trouble-maker whose name he later learned, Gondra, was taunting a rough-looking fellow who had stopped to buy a bottle of cane liquor for the road. The fellow had ignored Gondra's taunts, which therefore gradually increased in intensity. Moreira took the bit from his horse's mouth and hung the bag of corn around its neck for it to eat, and while he waited for the storekeeper to bring him a piece of meat for Cacique, he decided to stop Gondra from picking a fight.

What happened next shows the enormous sway that Moreira exer-cised over the people around him.

xii

Gondra believed that Moreira was there to enjoy the fun, and despite the calming words that Moreira spoke to him, he continued to insult the rough-looking stranger in uglier and uglier terms. The stranger, too, believed that Moreira was on Gondra's side, and by this time he was having difficulty suppressing an angry reaction to the stream of insults. Nonetheless, he paid for his bottle of cane liquor without opening his mouth, and walked away unhurriedly, measuring Gondra up and down with a deadly look.

Gondra laughed uproariously, and turning to Moreira, he said:

"Better step aside, partner, or this fellow with the cane liquor might just eat you up!"

The rough-looking stranger had had enough. He tossed the bottle into the yard of the pulpería and drew his facón.

"If you're a man," he said to Gondra, tilting his head toward the door, "come out here so I can have the pleasure of splitting you open," and turning to the others, especially Moreira, he added: "And that goes for the rest of you bunch of cowards, too. Any that wants to fight can come on . . . or *all* of you, one at a time."

Moreira had his back to the counter of the pulpería and was leaning against it. He didn't budge, and nor did anyone else. Everyone there assumed that the famous Juan Moreira would accept the challenge to fight.

"Come on out, coward," shouted the challenger, now standing outside. "Come out, and I'll teach you to laugh at people."

Gondra started out the door, but he was a worthless gaucho, the sort that they call "all mouth," and the challenger's resolute attitude struck fear into his heart. He stopped in the doorway.

"I knew you were all mouth," shouted the challenger at Gondra. "So where's your pal who came to take your part? Somebody else come out, or I'm going in after you."

At that point, without even looking out at the challenger, Moreira took Gondra firmly by the arm.

"This isn't anybody's fight but yours," he said. "Now that you've started it, you'd better go finish it, because if you don't, you'll never hear the end of it."

At first, Gondra thought that Moreira was joking, but one look in our hero's eyes wiped the smile off his worthless face. As much as he feared the challenger standing outside, he feared Moreira more, especially when Moreira, too, drew his facón, and said:

"Now, get out there, or I'll have your guts all over the floor."

Feeling the sharp point of Moreira's blade against his back, Gondra pulled his own weapon and moved toward the stranger. Once the fight had started, Gondra looked a little better, giving as good as he got, but within a few minutes his arm and his chest were bloody, and he began to back away. He stopped when his felt the point of Moreira's facón between his shoulder blades.

"Get back in there, coward!" snarled Moreira. "If he kills you, it's only fair."

Gondra leapt forward just as the stranger, glancing over at Moreira, dropped his guard momentarily. One moment was enough. Gondra's facón slipped between the stranger's fourth and fifth ribs, straight into his heart, killing him instantly.

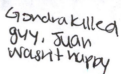
Gondra killed guy, Juan wasn't happy

Gondra was overjoyed and seemed to expect congratulations from Moreira, but he didn't get any. Instead, Moreira sheathed his knife and gave the killer a kick that sent him stumbling against the counter of the pulpería.

"You make me want to throw up," he said over his shoulder as went to his dappled bay, replaced its bit, mounted, and left at a gallop.

After galloping a few minutes, Moreira slowed his horse to a trot and turned in the direction of the district of Cañuelas, where he had a friend from whom he hoped to obtain information about Vicenta and little Juan. What awaited Moreira in Cañuelas, however, was further misfortune, as we shall see.

The gaucho traveled all day, taking the normal precautions, resting and feeding his horse every two hours or so, while he lay on the grass with Cacique and pondered his fate. At one point he even considered going to live among the Indians, but no, he had to find out what had become of his family. His friend Doctor Alsina might be able to help him, but how could Moreira inform him of the situation? He did not trust the mail, suspecting that any letter he sent to Alsina would surely be opened and probably destroyed, never to reach its destination.

The gaucho passed the night and the next morning in similar meditations, arriving, by the end of the afternoon, which was Sunday, at a pulpería full to overflowing with rambunctious rural men who had been there for hours throwing the *taba*, betting on horse races, and drinking cane liquor with lemon and sugar, the classic drink of the countryside.[2] The storekeeper had gotten into a wonderful good humor filling glasses as fast as he could, and every so often one of the celebrants picked up the guitar to play and sing some gaucho ditty in a woozy, nasal voice. Practically no one left the pulpería that day until all his money was spent. A gaucho's tirador is studded with silver coins, normally, if he can afford that luxury, and on the afternoon in question, many of those in attendance had divested themselves even of that most basic adornment.

Our fun-loving hero could not resist a scene like that, and soon he was tying the dappled bay to the hitching post, using his usual slip knot in case he had to make a quick getaway.

"God keep all good people!" he shouted to the happy crowd.

---

2. Taba is a gambling game of "heads" or "tails," played with the knuckle bone of a cow or sheep.

"Viva Juan Moreira!" they shouted in reply, and ten or twelve of them approached him immediately to shake his hand of offer him a drink. Some pounded on his back and shoulders, and others stretched out a finger jabbed the air, as if fencing with knives.

Moreira responded avidly to their shows of affection and friendship and shook everybody's hand, but he turned down all offers of liquor, saying:

"I've got to take care of my family first, and I'll be right back."

Going to the counter, he asked for hay for his horse and a piece of meat for Cacique, then took these outside to where "his family" waited, the horse with twitching ears, and the little dog still mounted on the saddle, wagging its tail and barking.

xiii

Moreira lifted his faithful little friend off the saddle and petted him for a moment before placing him on the ground beside the dappled bay and stooping to cut the dog's meat into bite size pieces. Then, after checking that both animals had water, he returned to the pulpería.

Inside, there was one gaucho who sat sullenly on a wine barrel in a corner with his arms crossed, taking no part in the rowdy welcome that the other men gave Moreira. Moreira had not noticed him, or at least, had not seemed to, and everyone else ignored him completely. This man's name was Juan Córdoba. He had something of a reputation as a fighter, and Moreira's fame made him jealous. Just that morning he had been saying that if Moreira had all the police frightened, it was simply because he had never met his match among them.

"But he doesn't have a match," protested the others. "Some say the devil himself fights at his side."

"The devil doesn't scare me," Córdoba had boasted in reply. "The day he crosses *my* path, the devil won't save him."

The others had ignored his boast and absorbed themselves cheerfully in the pastimes we've already described, which explains

Córdoba's defiant attitude when Moreira arrived at the pulpería some hours later.

Now Moreira was surrounded by celebrants, accepting the drinks offered him on all sides, and trying to answer the shower of questions he was asked all at once. Soon he was ordering drinks for the house. Only Córdoba did not raise a glass to toast him.

"Won't you have a drink, friend?" Moreira asked him, finally noticing Córdoba's refusal to touch the glass of liquor that had been served for him and remained, untouched, on the counter of the pulpería.

"I only drink what I buy myself," answered the other in distinctly surly tones. "And I have money to pay, thank God."

"You're luckier than me, then," said Moreira with a frown and a shake of his head, refusing to be provoked, "because I can't seem to get a break. Whether it's because of God or the Devil, I wouldn't know."

Looking at the ceiling, and shaking his head again, Moreira moved away from Córdoba, who remained seated on the wine barrel. The hum of voices returned after having been temporarily hushed during the exchange. Someone picked up the guitar, and Moreira sat down to hear about the horse races run earlier that day. More drinks were served, and more. Only the taciturn Córdoba drank nothing.

At that point one of the men picked up the guitar decorated with multicolored ribbons and held it out to Moreira, asking him to sing some décimas.

"No friend, I can't sing anymore. All I can do is cry."

"But a man's got to get that stuff off his chest," said another gaucho, and so much did they beg and insist, that finally Moreira took the guitar, and began the sort of finger picking that accompanies the saddest, more beautiful melodies of the pampa.

A general applause and movement to refill glasses greeted Moreira's first chords, and for as much as ten minutes he sang nothing, his left hand traveling up and down the fret board of the guitar, creating vaguely disconnected chords and interludes, his right hand playing rolls and rich bass notes vibrant with melancholy. Moreira's head was down and his eyes, closed, as he played. Then the vaguely disconnected chords came together, and the gaucho lifted his handsome face and opened his eyes, which seemed to see nothing in the room, but only some vision from his overflowing heart, and sang three perfect décimas.

However rude some of their customs and surroundings, gauchos have a very poetic sensibility and a special love of verse improvisation.

The décimas that Moreira sang on the Sunday afternoon in question were written down by someone who was present, and later recited to me during one of my fact-finding trips to Navarro. They are exquisitely refined, following the age-old poetic game of "glossing" a famous quotation, in this case a quotation from *Don Quixote*: "Come, elusive death . . ." These precisely rhymed ten-line stanzas are all the more remarkable in view of the fact that Moreira may have been improvising or adapting them on the spot. Moreira's metaphors were simple and unforced. He was a dying tree, its roots blasted, never more to flower or bear fruit, awaiting 'elusive death,' that must finally come to relieve his suffering. Anyone who might doubt his desire for death should take the full measure of his pain, and doubt no more. Come, elusive death!

Las décimas de Moreira

Presa el alma del dolor
con el corazón marchito,
soy como el árbol maldito
que no da fruta ni flor.
Muerte, ven a mi clamor,
que en ti mi esperanza anida;
ven, acaba con me vida,
ven en silencio profundo,
como mi dolor al mundo,
ven, muerte, tan escondida.

Quizá el mundo en su embriaguez,
sin conocer mi martirio,
tenga mi afán por delirio
hijo de la insensatez.
Y al ver mi ardiente avidez
por acabar de existir,
los que estiman el venir
como suprema ventura
dirán que es en mí locura.
¿Por qué el placer de morir?

¡Ah! si vieran la inclemencia
con que en mí el dolor goza,
que hoja por hoja destroza

las flores de mi existencia,
comprendieran la vehemencia
con que anhelo tu venida.
Ven, muerte, tan escondida,
que no te sienta venir,
y el gusto de verte herir
no me vuelva a dar la vida.

All eyes were on Moreira as he sang. No one spoke or moved, even during the musical interludes of several minutes between verses, when the singer was mentally improvising the next perfectly-rhymed décima. Not a few gauchos had softly wiped tears out of their eyes with the backs of their leathery hands. Moreira's emotion vibrated through them. It was something they could relate easily to their own lives. Even Córdoba at last got off the wine barrel and moved toward the singer. When the third décima was concluded, Moreira left the last, wrenching guitar notes hanging in the air. The silence lingered a while.

The man who had requested the décimas thanked Moreira with a glass of cane liquor, and said simply:

"This is good for what ails you."

Moreira's full black beard glistened with dew drops, and the lines of suffering graven on his brow were deep, indeed. He accepted the glass of cane liquor and drained it, in one motion.

Córdoba had been watching Moreira sing as if in a trance, his glass of liquor forgotten in his hand. When Moreira drank, so did he, then returned to his solitary perch on the barrel. Soon the party was back in full swing.

Now the men convinced Moreira to describe his battle with Leguizamón, blow by blow, including the various incidents and exchanges that led up to it, all of which he did with the greatest simplicity and humility.

"And it's too bad he died," said Moreira, "because he left a wife and children and, besides, I hear he wasn't a bad sort, really. It was his job to fight with me, after all. There was no personal dispute between us. We had never met before the day I killed him. God knows that I have never fought except as a last resort."

"That's the way the world is, though," piped up Córdoba from his wine barrel. "We're like moths to the flame, fluttering, fluttering, and finally frying. It happens even to those who think they are too brave to fight."

Moreira ignored Córdoba, although he well understood his intent, and spoke to the other men.

"Death holds no terrors for me. If I haven't taken my own life, it's only because I think that my wife and son still need me."

"Let's leave sad stories for tomorrow!" shouted a man with the heavy voice of blind drunkenness. "Tonight we'll each dance a malambo, and tomorrow we'll pray for the dead! Storekeeper, a round of drinks for the house. Let's drink to the health of Juan Moreira, a man who is more gaucho than the devil himself, by God!"

And so saying, he pulled a roll of silver coins out of his tirador and banged them on the counter. The storekeeper and his assistants hurried to fill dozens of glasses, including the empty glass that Córdoba had left on the counter. Córdoba leapt off his barrel.

"I said I only drink what I pay for myself," he said angrily. "And I don't drink to anyone's health unless I feel like it."

Moreira sighed but kept his mouth shut. This fellow seemed set on a ruckus, and he really wanted to leave the party, and the district of Navarro, without having to use his knife again. He drank his glass as "one for the road" and took his leave of the group. He wanted to cross into the district of Cañuelas unobserved, before dawn.

Now Córdoba sealed his own fate.

"Fear is prudent, don't you see," he said in a theatrically loud voice, with a broad wink to the storekeeper. "That's how even the toughest gauchos become as gentle as little lambs."

Moreira, who had taken two steps out the door, turned around slowly and came back.

"I swore I'd leave this nice party without spilling blood," he said, "but I didn't swear I'd allow myself to be insulted by a mangy cur like you."

Córdoba now took the glass of liquor from the counter and raised it, as if to toast.

"I am no Leguizamón," he said the same theatrical tone, "nor am I a man whom you can intimidate. I'm Juan Córdoba, you've heard of me."

"You won't need a name for long," snarled Moreira.

Córdoba stepped back from the counter, drew his facón, and threw the entire contents of his glass directly in Moreira's face.

Moreira shook his head and roared. That is not intended to be metaphorical. The sound that came out of his mouth bore no resemblance to a human voice. It was the explosive release of the most powerful frustrations, like a blast of scorching wind straight from hell.

It was the last sound Córdoba ever heard. Although dozens of men crowded the room, the fight happened so fast that, afterward, it was difficult to reconstruct, and *fight* hardly seemed the right word, anyway. Here are the basics. Moreira pounced close to Córdoba in a fraction of a second, and in the next fraction, drove the most powerful facón thrust imaginable toward Córdoba's belly. Córdoba parried the thrust, or tried to, but he just wasn't strong enough to save himself. Córdoba's parry failed to deflect Moreira's facón in the slightest, at best, Córdoba was able to slow Moreira's facón as it went in. In the last fraction of a second, Moreira pushed Cordoba back against the counter with such force that the sharp tip of his blade got stuck in a vertebra. When Moreira tried to withdraw his facón, he had to push back on the wounded man's chest and finally sent him stumbling back against the barrel where he'd sat all night. Córdoba crashed to the floor and died without uttering a word.

Moreira waved his bloody knife in a fit of frustration, then walked out the door, still holding the weapon in his hand and muttering:

"Everywhere I go, it's the same story."

"Don't worry," said the man who bought the last round and toasted his health. "It was him or you. He had it out for you. "

Moreira left quickly and galloped for most of a mile before he realized that he still had his blood-encrusted facón in his hand, and Cacique was running beside the dappled bay asking to be lifted up to the saddle.

xiv

Córdoba's demise had made a profound impression on Moreira, whose idea, when he turned around and reentered the pulpería, had been merely to rough up the loudmouth. His reaction had been automatic, and he had killed without intending to, hardly aware that he was killing.

He rode all night and all of the next day in the direction of Cañuelas, arriving at about eleven o'clock at night, when the streets of the town were deserted. Moreira was not known there, and he rode calmly into town and stopped after a few blocks to knock at the door of a thatch-roofed house surrounded by a bit of land belonging to the brother of Julián.

"Who's there?" came the answer, through the unopened door. In pampa towns like Cañuelas, it isn't wise to open the door without precautions when a knock comes in the middle of the night.

"It's me, friend Santiago," said Moreira more quietly.

There was an excited bustle inside, the door opened, and the two men greeted each other like long-lost brothers, although they had, in fact, never met.

"Julián has told us all about you," said Santiago, "but we had no idea where you were. Some have been saying that you're dead."

"I've come to ask you for a favor," said his guest.

Moreira met Santiago's wife Marta, who also received him just as warmly as Santiago had done. When the two men were seated inside passing the mate gourd, Moreira explained why he had come:

"I need you to get in touch with Julián for me and ask him to learn what people are saying in Matanzas about my wife and son. I'm planning to go far away, but I can't leave without news of them. I'd go myself, but I would be recognized immediately."

"At dawn, I'll go find Julián and round up several spare mounts for him," replied Santiago. "He'll go to Matanzas and back like an express rider. I'd leave right now, but I'm waiting for Marta's brother, who isn't due back until tomorrow morning."

Moreira saw to his animals, said a polite goodnight, and fell into the soft, clean bed that the couple offered him, probably their own. In seconds, it seemed, he was deeply asleep.

"It's incredible that he can sleep so soundly with the life he's had to lead," Santiago commented to his wife.

The life of an outlaw had changed Juan Moreira, as he himself had noticed the day before. He was getting used to killing. There was a time when Moreira might toss and turn all night worrying about a friend's bad luck. Now he could sleep like a baby following, or preceding, the most hair-raising events imaginable. On this occasion, he slept straight through the night and awoke only when the sun was already high in the sky.

Marta informed him that Santiago had already left in search of Julián. In the meantime, her brother was there, should Moreira need something. It was better that he stay out of sight, because the Justice of the Peace of Cañuelas, Nicolás González, was an honest and effective lawman.

After a full night's sleep, the first in many weeks, Moreira was in a good mood. Soon he would have news of his family. Reflexively, he readied the dappled bay, which he'd unsaddled the night before for the first time in as many weeks, and took Cacique inside. The day passed almost happily. Moreira ate his roasted meat with a good appetite and even sang and played the guitar some, to the delight of Marta, who found the famous outlaw Juan Moreira to be an unexpectedly fun-loving sort, worthy of her best liquor.

By ten o'clock, Marta was nodding off, and Moreira said that he should get some sleep, as well. He very politely refused the offer of the clean, soft bed, however, and instead slept outside under the stars, in the position that my readers can now well imagine: face down on his poncho, with his head resting on his crossed arms and his weapons under his hands. Cacique curled up beside his master, and in ten minutes both were asleep.

It was about four o'clock in the morning when Cacique's bark brought Moreira to his feet with a cocked trabuco in each hand. Santiago's house was on the edge of town, and in the thinning pre-dawn darkness along the horizon the gaucho detected a cloud of dust. It was enough to indicate possibly a dozen horses. Moreira continued to watch intently while Cacique stopped barking, sat, and looked at him quizzically. After a few more minutes, Moreira began to see the horses that had raised the dust, eleven of them, but only two riders.

Moreira's frown relaxed, and he smiled. It was Santiago and Julián, no doubt, with no fewer than nine spare mounts, and they were moving very fast. Another ten minutes and they had arrived.

Julián and Moreira, two tough gauchos, greeted each other like lovers. Enveloping each other in a giant abrazo, they kissed and laughed and grinned and said nothing, while Santiago busied himself putting up the horses and building up the fire to heat more water. Clearly, there would be a lot of mate drunk that morning as Moreira told Julián everything that had happened in Navarro, right through killing Córdoba more or less by mistake, and concluding with the reason that he had come to Cañuelas.

"I've got to know about Vicenta and the boy, Julián," he said, "and nobody is more gaucho than you."

"I'll bring you news of them," swore Moreira's true friend, "if I have to go find it at the end of the earth. I'll leave as soon as it's dark, and then, watch my speed!"

The men spent the morning drinking mate and laughing, principally, at Julián's countless jokes and droll stories. In the afternoon, Santiago's friends began to drop over, and weren't they amazed to find themselves in the presence of the famous Juan Moreira! Even the men who had known Moreira in earlier years, and who invariably liked him, looked at him now rather in awe. Just at dark, Julián set off for Matanzas on a fast horse with a remount equally fast, galloping away like a messenger entrusted with the most urgent kind of news.

Moreira was ready to continue the party until Julián came back, but it was not to be. Instead, the events that ensued in Cañuelas added powerfully to Moreira's fame in a way reminiscent of the old tales of chivalry. I can guarantee the veracity of my account because it was related to me by a gentleman of sterling reputation, Nicolás González, who was the Justice of the Peace in Cañuelas at the time.

Not long after Julián's departure, someone took Moreira word that Justice González already knew of his presence in town and had decided to arrest him.

"They've warned the judge that it won't be easy," said the bringer of these bad tidings, "but he says that for that very reason the attempt must be made, and he's sent to Navarro for reinforcements."

Santiago and Marta lost their high spirits instantaneously, but not our hero, who was quite pleased to see how much he was now feared by so-called lawmen.

"Oh, there's going to be a scuffle," he said, as light-heartedly as if he were going to be a spectator rather than the one in a ten-to-one fight.

Despite Santiago's repeated attempts to convince him to escape while there was still time, Moreira refused. Instead, he told the man to go back with a message for the police captain: the reinforcements would not help, but he would wait for them to arrive anyway.

"Come back and tell me when they're ready," said Moreira, "and they won't have to come look for me."

That night Moreira retired early, again, as the night before, to sleep on the ground beside his horse, and again he slept well. Santiago and Marta, on the other hand, hardly slept at all, expecting the police to surround the house at any moment. Nothing happened, however, to disturb anyone's slumber or provoke the shrill bark of the little dog Cacique.

The next morning Santiago slipped out to do a bit of reconnaissance and returned confirming that the Justice of the Peace had ordered that the police take Moreira dead or alive. They awaited only the arrival of reinforcements. On Santiago's heals came a townsman reporting that the reinforcements from Navarro had now arrived and joined the Cañuelas police in the square at the center of town.

"Let me not keep them waiting," said Moreira, beginning immediate preparations. "Those cowards from Navarro may not stay around if they can say they didn't see me anywhere. Besides, I don't want them to find me in this house."

Just as he always did at such a moment, Moreira methodically checked his weapons, especially the mechanism and ammunition of his two trabucos with their short, flaring bronze barrels, then mounted, putting Cacique behind him, and set off for the center of town at a trot. When he got there, the captain of the Cañuelas police had just ordered his fourteen troopers to mount their horses. Little did he suspect that the man he had been charged to bring in dead or alive had already come to pay him a call.

Such a large expedition had created much excitement and attracted many onlookers, so Moreira, whose face was not well known in Cañuelas, easily rode into the crowd of people and horses and, making his way through, approached the police captain at the head of the departing column.

"I can save you some trouble, captain," he said. "Moreira is not where they say. And I'm not saying that he ever was, but he left there ten minutes ago."

"If you know anything about Moreira," replied the captain, "then you'll have to come along."

Meanwhile, the four police reinforcements from Navarro had recognized Moreira, but instead of raising the alarm, they took advantage of that piece of intelligence to save their own skins by moving to the rear of the column.

"It's no use, captain," laughed our hero, "because you'll never catch him, I can promise you that."

"See here," said the captain, who had begun to think that this fellow was simply trying to create a delay, "tell me where Moreira is right now or you'll find yourself with your head in the stocks."

By this time several other people in the crowd had recognized Moreira and the news began to ripple through the crowd, too late to help the captain, however.

"All right then," replied our hero, still laughing, now with his hand on his chest. "He's right here!"

And before the captain could react, Moreira spurred his horse forward against the captain's mount, knocking the captain to the ground, where he writhed helplessly entangled in the straps of his scabbard, try-ing to get up, as his horse bolted away. The four reinforcements from Navarro bolted, too, as Moreira faced the remaining ten police troopers.

"Fire!" shouted the captain, finally on his feet and drawing his sword. "Kill the bandit!"

Several of his men obeyed, but they did so virtually without aim-ing, in the manner that makes firearms such ineffective weapons among our countrymen who seldom use them. Moreira, who, as we know, aims his shots well, indeed, put the reins in his teeth and pulled both his trabucos, cocking them loudly at the same time.

"Get him, get him, get him!" shouted the captain, bravely lunging at the mounted Moreira with his sword.

Moreira watched the captain with one eye and kept his horse in motion to avoid the slashing saber, while extending his trabucos toward the ten soldiers and aiming with the other eye.

There was a very loud bang, composed of two practically simulta-neous explosions. Smoke and horses rolled in the dusty street, where two soldiers lay torn in several places by the flying lead. Three of their comrades turned their horses and fled at a dead run, while the remaining five struggled to control their startled mounts. Given that these mounts were of the worthless sort generally issued to the soldiers and police of our republic, it was not an easy job, and thus Moreira had time to reload his trabucos, which he did with incredible rapidity. Moreira's trabucos were old-fashioned muzzle-loaders. To reload, he took two paper cartridges containing powder and shot from his tirador, pushed them into the two barrels, and pounded the butts of the two weapons on the front of his saddle so that the cartridges dropped into place. By the time that the captain had regrouped the remaining policemen for another charge at Moreira, he was cocking his trabucos again.

Moreira aimed with both arms, and again the very loud bang resounded in the dusty town square. Several more soldiers—it was hard to tell how many amid the smoke and confusion—bit the dirt and the rest galloped off, abandoning the field completely to Juan Moreira, who was laughing so hard that he seemed about to fall off his horse.

The captain, on the other hand, was white with shame and tremu-lous with rage. Again he lunged suicidally at Moreira, who had no trouble staying away from him. Putting away his trabucos, he looked at the brave young captain sympathetically.

"Get on out of here," he said, "I've no quarrel with you. Take word of the disaster."

Further humiliated by Moreira's jocular air, the captain continued to slice the air with this saber. A bit wearily, the gaucho dismounted and wrapped his poncho of vicuña wool around his left arm, while the crowd, which generally shared Moreira's fondness for the young captain, braced itself for the sad spectacle of his trying to fight the famous Juan Moreira one-on-one.

But Moreira had done enough killing for one day. Even though the captain had a heavy cavalry saber twice as long at Moreira's facón, the gaucho was in complete control of the situation. Smiling the famous smile that people saw on his face during mortal combat, he opened his arms to present a big target. The captain lunged, and Moreira dodged, deflecting the sword with his poncho. As the captain dove into the dirt, Moreira tapped him on the head with the flat of his facón, as if to say "you're it."

"Kill *me* then, now for God's sake!" said the young man, getting up.

"No," said Moreira, "you've got a family, I guess, and there's no need for you to die over something so stupid. You followed your orders. You stood your ground against Juan Moreira. That's pretty good."

The young captain panted and said nothing. Moreira saw that his reasoning was useless. He smiled and nodded as if confiding a secret to himself. He opened his arms wide again, and the captain lunged. He lunged with great courage and all the strength that remained in his body straight at the deadliest fighter to tread Argentine soil in decades, and Moreira loved him for it. Almost delicately, he slipped to the side and, with a sliding movement, swept the poor captain's legs out from under him. The captain fell on his back, knocking the breath out of him, leaving him helpless on the ground.

Moreira wrenched the captain's sword from his hand and threw it across the unpaved square. The crowd shuttered, expecting that he would now finish the captain in the traditional manner, with a single broad cut from ear to ear. Those who did not turn away saw something quite different.

"Sorry about that," said Moreira to the captain, and he flipped his poncho playfully against the fallen man's head, as if at the conclusion of a pillow fight.

Then he walked across the square to where his dappled bay horse stood, having withdrawn to a prudent distance, and then waited, with Cacique pacing back and forth on the saddle to keep everyone away until Moreira's return. The square of Cañuelas was still full of people, all watching our hero more or less openmouthed.

"Gentlemen, call a doctor," he said, and then, with a shake of his head, "and probably a priest. I can't stay to help, because I have a lot to do."

He spoke not in the taunting tones that he sometimes employed but quite matter-of-factly. And then, without a trace of hurry, he reined around and rode away at a walk as the flabbergasted towns-people watched in silence, completely under his sway. After he disappeared around a corner, his laugh came wafting back.

The people of our countryside and small towns have an enormous respect for physical courage, and more so when joined to noble and humanitarian sentiments. Many of the men in the square that day would have been willing to fight as Moreira did, because in that sense he is a good specimen of his beautiful race. Fewer, many fewer would have spared the young captain's life, however.

Moreira returned to Santiago's house, for he still awaited news from Julián. Santiago and Marta, who had heard the shooting, could hardly believe their eyes when the gaucho came riding calmly back, as if returning from a friendly visit.

"Get out of here, friend, for God's sake!" protested Santiago. The army is around here looking for conscripts, and you can't fight *them* the way you do the police."

Moreira finished tying his horse in spite of Santiago's protests.

"I can and I will fight them," he said, "just the way I fought that pack of cowards today. Comadre, a gourd of mate if you would be so kind. . . ."

And he proceeded to narrate the afternoon's events for the benefit of Santiago, who listened with round eyes.

"Nobody is more gaucho than you, Juan Moreira," marveled Santiago. "But now, best leave. Courage is wonderful, but prudence has its place. Pain is faithful but luck is fickle, as they say. Best leave, and when Julián gets back, I'll let him know where to find you, how's that?"

"Don't worry about me," replied Moreira as Marta handed him the mate gourd. "I'm going to wait for Julián right here, even if he comes with an entire battalion of devils right behind him, as long as you don't mind, of course."

And so our hero settled in to wait for Julián, while all Cañuelas buzzed with commentary on the astonishing combat that had taken place that day, when Juan Moreira single-handedly slammed a rein-forced party of mounted police and then pardoned the life of the widely liked young captain.

XV

Two days of waiting followed. Moreira did not seem restless, but Santiago and Marta hardly slept a wink. Not until the early morning hours of the third day did Cacique's shrill bark give warning of approaching horses. It was Julián with several remounts, as Moreira recognized when the little dog's barking shifted from warning to welcome.

One look at Julián's face told the whole story. Moreira noticed a tear in his friend's eye, and he saw there the realization of his worst nightmare. Julián had been dreading this moment, trying for hours on end to formulate the right words with which to tell his friend the most awful news.

"Aw hell," he said, "when it rains, it pours. At least that's what they say."

Moreira's head fell limply on his chest, and he sat motionless trying to compose himself. Julián sat down at his side and waited. Finally, our hero raised his tear-streaked face.

"Okay," he said. "I'm ready now."

And so Julián told what he had learned in Matanzas.

Vicenta had been put out on the street with little Juan and led to believe that both her father and her husband were dead. She went home to find her house in complete ruin, the animals gone, the crops trampled, all their worldly possessions plundered, leaving not so much as a bench to sit on. Nor did she have a crumb to give Juancito, who was getting sick. She knocked on the doors of her friends and found them all closed to her because the Justice of the Peace had declared that "anyone who aided the bandit's wife would be considered his accomplice and held accountable before the law." Then "the law" had moved in like a pack of wolves to finish the job. Vicenta's ordeal had left her gaunt and desperate, but she was still a beautiful woman, and all the employees of the local courthouse took an opportunistic interest in her. Perhaps "circling vultures" describes them better than "wolves." But Vicenta would have nothing of it. She sent Francisco's replacement packing with fire in her eyes when the new Assistant Justice for her neighborhood dropped by to offer her protection and affection.

Moreira listened, sitting as silent and as still as a bronze statue, the tears still running down his cheeks.

Vicenta went often to visit her father's grave, where she sat and cried for hours, and she asked just as often to be told where her husband had been buried, but the lawmen just laughed. They said that Moreira's body had been left for carrion and eaten by wild animals. Vicenta could hardly get a piece of black cloth with which to dress in mourning and thus honor the memory of her father and her husband. She went from place to place imploring a bite of food for little Juancito, without success. Meanwhile the weather turned colder, and she did not even have fuel for a fire. It seemed that if the child did not starve it would soon die of exposure, and at that point the new Assistant Justice paid her another visit, renewing his generous offer. Truly desperate, she nonetheless refused him a second time and made up her mind to die rather than submit to his vile propositions.

At that point, a ray of hope appeared. Her compadre Giménez returned from taking a herd of cattle to market, a trip of several weeks, to offer Vicenta what seemed her salvation and little Juan's. But the compadre, whose responsibilities were greater than anyone else's because of the sacramental relationship that bound him to Moreira and Vicenta, turned out the be the worst traitor of all. He took up where the new Assistant Justice had left off, assuring her that Moreira was dead. She was free and in need. Now she needed to think of herself. Vicenta listened to his proposition in a daze, her mind weakened by hunger and fatigue. And of course, insisted Giménez, she must think of her child, who would probably die unless she found someone to take care of them both. Like an automaton, thinking only for her child if she was thinking at all, Vicenta accepted his "kind" proposition.

So the treacherous compadre, who well knew that Moreira was alive, installed himself in Moreira's house, and that night Vicenta and Juancito devoured their roasted meat almost without chewing it, they were so hungry. Then Vicenta collapsed and slept deeply for the first time in weeks, not fearing, for once, that she might awake with her little child dead in her arms.

When Julián reached this point in the story, Moreira finally interrupted it. He roared like a bull, shook his head violently, and then pressed it between his hands.

"Water!" he screamed. "My head is on fire!"

Santiago ran and brought a bucket of water, Moreira got on his knees to put the top of his head in it, and he stayed that way for three minutes. When he sat up, his long black hair gradually drenched his upper body with the cooling liquid, and Moreira tied a handkerchief around his forehead to keep the water out of his eyes. The trick had worked. His deadly calm had been restored, and he seemed to be out of tears.

"Go on, friend Julián," the gaucho said quietly. "Don't leave anything out. I've got to hear it all, so I can know just how slowly to kill that bastard."

Julián proceeded with his tale of woe.

Vicenta and Juancito had lacked for nothing after that first night. Little by little the child recovered his strength and the mother resigned herself to the new situation. The neighbors saw Giménez defying the court order not to give material aid to Moreira's wife, so they approved his actions. From time to time, Vicenta asked Giménez to find out where the authorities had buried Moreira's body, and he always promised to, but never did. Giménez did dote on Juancito, though, and Vicenta had to appreciate that. Well, one day Giménez had to take some cattle all the way to the city of Buenos Aires. He would be gone for a good while, weeks, and he left her with money to buy everything she might need in his absence.

The new Assistant Justice had been waiting for this moment to renew his disgusting advances toward Vicenta, but again she rejected him, and this time, more scornfully than the last.

"Don't dare even insinuate that again in this house," she declared.

"Do you think that Giménez can protect you against the law?" replied the scoundrel.

"I've done nothing wrong and have no reason to fear the law," insisted Vicenta.

She was mistaken, of course, if she really believed that she had nothing to fear. This particular lawman meant to have her for himself, and her resistance only maddened him and provoked him to greater efforts. The so-called lawmen of the pampa aren't accustomed to taking "no" for an answer. The jackal told Vicenta that her cohabitation with Giménez was illicit because the two were not properly married. He might be compelled to arrest her for that or, at least, take her child into custody because she was obviously an unfit mother. At that, Vicenta went at him, but he didn't hesitate to rebuff her with blows, and he threatened to beat the child, too, if he didn't get his way. He left saying that he'd be back tomorrow night.

Vicenta felt very alone in the world. She spent the night in a panic, holding Juancito in her arms, possessed by the fear that, if she dozed off, someone would steal him away from her. Not until morning did she actually sleep. There are times when the morning light comes like a comforting friend to banish the fantastic nightmares that have tormented us in the dark. She awoke an hour before noon, dressed, and left the house leading her child by the hand. She had nowhere else to go but merely fled the house because she regarded it as the place of maximum danger, the place where her nemesis had promised to return. Toward nightfall, she went back to the house to get a blanket, because she intended to sleep in the open air, away from the house. To her great relief, she found her compadre's horses outside the house.

Who was the worse coward? It wasn't clear. When Vicenta told Giménez that she expected the Assistant Justice that night, he immediately took Vicenta and Juancito to his own house. And the lawman prudently decided to wait until Giménez went away again before returning to his project of seduction, if one can call it that.

Julián paused, with the sensation that Moreira had spoken. Moreira's mouth was moving, but no sound was coming out of it. Julián thought for a moment, then continued a little more slowly, describing his own actions.

"So, when I found how things stood," he said, "I went to the Giménez place and pretended to know nothing about you or about anything else. Sure enough, there was Vicenta, and she came out to greet me before I'd gotten off my horse."

Julián told how she had shown him Juancito, who was clinging to her skirts and was already a little man, and how she had cried bitterly on Julián's shoulder, for some minutes, remembering happier times. The treacherous compadre had turned pale, indeed, when he set eyes on Julián, suspecting, as was in fact the case, that he might be there on behalf of Juan Moreira. When Vicenta went to heat water for mate and the two men were alone, Giménez had asked about Moreira, giving his own version of events—too full of lies to warrant repeating— and begged Julián not to let Vicenta know that her husband was still alive. She would be terrified, Giménez assured Julián, thinking that Moreira would surely kill her for being unfaithful in his absence.

"I about killed him right then," said Julián, addressing Moreira directly. "But then I thought better of it. It wasn't my place, and I knew you'd want to do it, so I left him for you."

Julián couldn't resist horsewhipping him a little, though, as he went on to explain, and unfortunately Vicenta had come out with the mate gourd while he was horsewhipping the fool, and it had somewhat upset her. So Julián had said he only did it because Giménez had spoken ill of Juan Moreira while she was inside.

"Nobody wipes his mouth with the name of Juan Moreira," said Julián, quoting his own words with obvious relish, "as long as I'm on earth and he's far away."

Vicenta misinterpreted his words in just the way he had intended and burst into tears, forgetting totally about Giménez, who crept away to a safe distance, then got up and ran.

"Don't worry, I'm leaving," said Juan Moreira's true friend to Vicenta. "I won't disturb you anymore. I just wanted to see what had become of you."

"You are always welcome in my house," said Vicenta. "Come drink mate."

And that's when she told Julián the whole story that he had just related to Juan Moreira.

When Julián had concluded the story of what he learned in Matanzas, Moreira described his fight in the town square of Cañuelas. His friend scolded him for provoking the police and tempting fate. He might have gotten killed for nothing.

"You're right, and I won't do that anymore," said Moreira, "because now I have a reason to live again. If I let the police get me, I won't get to meet the new Assistant Justice of my neighborhood, for whom I have a special message, and I won't get to hear the man who was my compadre, and Vicenta's, plead for mercy before he dies, and that's something I don't want to miss."

His friends, noticing that Moreira's hand rested on his knife handle and that his eyes looked a bit crazed, said nothing. Moreira let out a thunderous oath and then seemed to lapse into a quasi-comatose state, though sitting upright with his eyes open. No one moved, until finally Moreira suddenly revived and stood up with the resolute air of a man who's decided on a course of action.

"I'll be on my way now, friends," he said. "I won't say too many good-byes, though, because something tells me we'll meet again."

"Watch out," said Julián, "because they say that the army's out looking for conscripts not far from here."

"You're right, and I don't want to fight them now," replied the gaucho, "so I'm going far away from here, and I'll stay away until they've forgotten all about me. Then, when they least expect it, I'll be back."

Julián kept his friend company during his preparations to depart, checking his weapons, feeding his horse, adjusting the bridle, and finally, tightening the cinch for a long, danger-filled journey. At last, he put Cacique behind the saddle and mounted.

"*Hasta la vista*," he said, and stuck his hand out to Julián. The rough hands of the two gauchos came together with a loud clap, and their handshake lasted a long time. Then Moreira wheeled his horse and was gone in the night.

Julián stood looking into the darkness until the sound of the dappled bay's hooves faded away to nothing. Then, half dead with fatigue, he lay down under the eaves of Santiago's house, mumbled something like "Watch his back, Lord," and seconds later, began to snore.

xvi

Our hero galloped like the wind cross-country and due west toward the frontier. He had taken the handkerchief from around his forehead, and his thick curls flew behind him like a pirate's flag. When the tireless dappled bay had covered countless miles and the pale dawn began to peek above the horizon, Moreira stopped and scanned the pampa for long minutes, trying to determine his location. He could see the frontier town patriotically named El Veinticinco de Mayo, where friendly Indians came to trade. At this "end of the earth," nobody knew Juan Moreira, perhaps not even by reputation.

So he turned south, toward nearby Fort San Carlos, where he had done national guard service years earlier, taking part in the glorious battle fought against Calfucurá, the famous chief who led five thousand savages—the battle that made valiant Coronel Borges into a national hero, as many of my readers will remember. Coming into sight of the fort, the gaucho finally stopped to rest his magnificent steed during the heat of the day. Then he continued to the locality called Tapera de Díaz, the ruins of a frontier ranch that didn't last, now the camp of a renegade Indian chief, Simón Coliqueo.

Just as his name was Spanish, Coliqueo's "tribe" was a motley mix of four hundred renegades, most of whom were Indians of some sort but many of whom were men like Moreira, who had been welcomed into Indian encampments and lived there semi-permanently. To neutralize the threat of Coliqueo's "tribe," the braves had been put on the army payroll, and to keep them camped at Tapera de Díaz, they also received army food rations. Naturally, they had become the laziest things in the world. Occasionally the military commander gave them permission to go out ostrich hunting, and when they come back with feathers that bring a fine price on the export market, certain sharp traders are there to profit from Indian foolishness. They trade feathers and skins worth hundreds of pesos for a bottle of gin or a few pounds of mate and sugar. Our frontier soldiers have a colorful term for those traders—bloodsuckers, they call them—but it must be recognized that contact with them and with our gallant military officers has notably civilized the savages.

The first thing that the Indians do after selling their ostrich feathers is get drunk. Very unlike payday in a civilized town, the encampments of the savages become quiet at that time, because they have all drunk to the point of stupefaction. What beautiful cases of alcoholism could modern science document at Tapera de Díaz! And the drunkest of them all was the chief Simón Coliqueo, for the simple reason that he had money to buy more bottles than any of his men.

This is the Godforsaken place to which Juan Moreira had come to hide until the authorities of Matanzas had forgotten about him. He impressed the Indians with his drinking. He went ostrich hunting with them and impressed them greatly with the way he sent the three *bolas* whirling through the air to tangle the legs of a fleeing bird. Moreira's saddle and bridle with their fancy silver trimmings were the utmost dream of many a renegade brave, and Moreira's music charmed these savage beasts utterly, making him their most pampered guest. They say that the Indian women liked Moreira even more than their men did. I wouldn't know. Moreira's heart was full of better things, and if he had any little idylls during his time at Tapera de Díaz, I have not heard about it. Nor will I try to find out.

Next to drinking, what Indians like best is gambling, and Moreira could easily beat them at that, too. His nimble fingers, shuffling and dealing a deck of cards, worked wonders with Lady Luck. He had already forgotten more about cards, in fact, than any Indian would ever know. Now, the savages bet the way they drink, to the last drop, and they don't like losing. After their money is gone, it's their gold-trimmed military cap, and the brave who's lost his kepi at cards is ready to kill, don't you know. Moreira, for his part, never lost at cards, at least with Indians, and more than once he had to pull out his knife to take care of some disagreeable problem that arose.

The Indians were impressed by that, too. Chief Coliqueo went so far as to tell Moreira that, if he stayed at Tapera de Díaz, he'd make him a captain and marry him into the tribe, a disgusting offer that the wily Moreira was careful not to disdain too openly. Coliqueo's friendship was too valuable to lose over the matter. Instead, Moreira planned a much more intelligent response.

Three months had passed, time enough for the authorities to lower their guard in Matanzas, time now to get the revenge for which his poor heart thirsted against his treacherous compadre and the new Assistant Justice of his old neighborhood. Our hero planned to take his leave of friend Simón and his tribe in a clever and profitable manner. Let's see the unforgettable way that he made it back to civilization!

Now, gambling happens most on the frontier when the paymaster comes. He doesn't come every month, by any means, either. And those tiny military salaries add up when they arrive many months in arrears. Moreira learned when the paymaster would be coming to Tapera de Díaz, and he began to execute his plan, spreading word that he wanted to sell his dappled bay horse with the silver-trimmed saddle and bridle.

Chief Coliqueo wanted them immediately, offering all the back pay that he expected to receive soon as well as seven mares, which he had been saving for meat. Moreira heaved a sigh, saying he'd wait for the paymaster before deciding. He had an itch to try his luck at cards, he said.

Wasn't the paymaster awaited fervently then! Chief Coliqueo looked at the dappled bay horse, and his mouth watered. He wanted to take it out for a ride, but the gaucho knew better than to let him. Finally, the paymaster arrived, the money was counted and recounted, and the big game was announced for that very evening.

In fact, there was a game in every tent that night, but everyone considered Chief Coliqueo's tent the place to be. Coliqueo wanted to start one-on-one with Moreira for high stakes, but our hero explained that he'd rather play with Coliqueo's captains first. So the chief let his captains start, and he watched as they lost their money, as each underwent a thorough fleecing. Even though there were fifteen men in the tent, all watching Moreira closely, his cleverness and dexterity were beyond them.

Coliqueo's captains kept losing all night and all the next day, stopping only so that Moreira could tend to his animals periodically, until they had lost all their money and their most valued possessions to boot. As darkness came on the second day, Coliqueo's tent was full of braves who were out of the game but stayed hoping to see Coliqueo win Moreira's dappled bay horse and silver-trimmed saddle and bridle. It was late by the time the last captain got up from the "card table," a large sheep fleece saddle in the middle of the tent.

Coliqueo sat down in his place, opposite Moreira, and put several fistfuls of silver pesos in front of him.

Before they began, Moreira stood up and said it was time to feed his horse, and, stepping out of the tent, he tightened his horse's cinch, put the bit in its mouth, and checked his weapons. The tent was surrounded by other horses, as well, because people on the frontier go everywhere, even if it's only a few hundred yards, on horseback. The Indians failed to notice the gaucho's astute move, which had nothing to do with cowardice. Our hero had no intention of turning over his dappled bay horse even if he lost at cards, while if he won, he could expect the Indians to be sore losers.

The game was simple, explained the gaucho after reentering the tent. One card to each player, the higher card wins.

Moreira then dealt two cards face down in front of Coliqueo, who pinned them to the table with his greedy eyes. Coliqueo's captains recently divested of their miserable possessions crowded avidly around the two players, completely blocking Moreira's way out of the tent. The gaucho invited them to come around for a better view. Ah gaucho! Little did the Indians suspect his finesse.

After he had stared at the two cards for a long time, Coliqueo's expression became even greedier, and he finally spoke:

"Card this playing, brother," he said, indicating one of the two cards with his finger, and he added "horse," because the back of the card had a picture of a horse.

Moreira turned the card over, a very high one! An electric current ran through the Indians, causing them to vibrate with happiness.

"Horse winning horse!" announced Coliqueo.

Moreira took the greasy deck and gently shuffled it, protractedly and almost absent-mindedly. Several times he had the cards virtually out of sight as he leaned back on an elbow to rest or rolled a cigarette, which he then let hang from his lip, and he continued to handle the cards. Meanwhile, the redskin ogled his high card but still sweated with impatience. To see him there, calmly enjoying Coliqueo's impatience, smiling, who would guess the position in which Moreira found himself?

Surrounded by fifteen angry savages who watched with rapt attention, Moreira continued to shuffle the cards. Then he quickly dealt himself one and turned it over for all to see. It was higher than Coliqueo's card.

The Indians gave an angry, menacing cry. Moreira's win would cost Coliqueo all his silver pesos and any hope of ever possessing the dappled bay.

"Christian cheating!" howled the Indian. "Me winning, wanting horse!"

"Christian cheating!" howled all Coliqueo's captains menacingly as Moreira gathered their chief's money.

This was the eventuality for which our hero had prepared so carefully.

"I have never cheated!" he declared, withdrawing toward the door of the tent. "Lady Luck was kind to me, that's all. Oh, and I'm a better player, too! And anyway," he continued, now in a very good mood, "my dappled bay horse is not for a thieving Indian to ride!"

"Me wanting horse," reiterated Coliqueo. "Thieving Christian!"

And jumping over the improvised card table, he attacked the gaucho, with his furious captains right behind him.

Instead of killing his host, which would have been bad manners, Moreira preferred to slice open the chief's forehead, immediately blinding him with the copious blood of a head wound. Then he was out of the tent, on his horse, and gone.

Coliqueo's captains fell over each other trying to get out of the tent, only to hear the gaucho's parting laughter echoing in their ears. They stood and waited while Moreira escaped, until Coliqueo finally emerged with his head wrapped in a dirty rag, cursing like a demon. Finally one of his better captains got the nerve to interrupt his chief and ask if they should follow the gaucho.

Of course they should! Coliqueo was inconsolable with the loss of the dappled bay horse that he already considered his. Kill that Christian, and bring him that horse! Coliqueo's best captain chose four braves to go with him, each with a remount for maximum speed, and they followed hot on Moreira's trail.

The gaucho was quite a few miles ahead by that time but moving more slowly because he had appropriated a small herd of Coliqueo's horses as he exited the encampment. Calculating that he had left the Indians far enough behind, he slowed further and turned in the direction of El Veinticinco de Mayo, the town that he had spied upon first arriving in the region of the Indian frontier. There he planned to sell Coliqueo's horses so that he would have some cash in his pocket when he got to Matanzas, where he was headed next.

When dawn came, he stopped to rest his horse for half an hour, then pushed on, herding Coliqueo's horses in front of him. He had hardly gone more than a few hundred yards when he heard Cacique growling behind him and knew instantly that the Indians had caught up with him. Standing in the stirrups and looking back, he could see five riders, and he knew them to be Indians because of the way they carried their lances.

Moreira stopped immediately, dismounted, and moved away from the little herd of horses that he'd been driving to market, so that his gunshots would not startle and scatter them. He calculated that, seeing him on foot, the Indians would charge without thinking twice, most especially as they outnumbered him five to one, the kind of odds that make Indians brave.

And that is exactly what they did, leveling their lances and galloping straight at him. Moreira cocked his two trabucos and held them under his poncho. He stood calmly and watched them come, closer, closer, until they were hardly five steps away, at which moment he extended both arms and fired both weapons simultaneously at the oncoming Indians.

The flying mass of lead knocked two of them backward off of their horses, whereupon the remaining three turned tail, completely terrorized by the unexpected reception. Away they raced until, at what they regarded a safe distance, almost out of sight, they finally stopped to see if the gaucho was following them.

Meanwhile, Moreira took a careful look at the Indians who were on the ground. One of them, who had taken the full discharge of two barrels into his chest, was already dead. The other was bleeding from several lesser wounds. Moreira let him be, gathered the horses of the fallen Indians, which were grazing nearby, added them to his small herd, and set off toward El Veinticinco de Mayo. He didn't worry about the Indians that he had left behind him. He knew that they wouldn't follow.

xvii

He arrived at the town late in the afternoon. Because these horses had not been branded, Indians not understanding property rights, Moreira had no trouble selling his small herd without the annoying paperwork usually involved in selling horses. Then he went to the pulpería, and soon enough, his troubles started again.

A local tough guy called Duck was bragging, when Moreira entered, about nothing in particular. Duck didn't need a special reason to brag, because he did it all the time, possibly to compensate for his silly nickname. Duck was one of those frontier gauchos who still wear the old *bota de potro*, the famous "colt boot" of the real old-timers, which, for the benefit of my urban readers, was the raw leather pulled off a colt's leg and onto a gaucho's foot, inside out, so that the hairy side is inside. The gaucho's toes normally stick out in a manner that any of my readers who has seen it will surely remember. The white leather dries on the gaucho's leg and shrinks tightly in place, splaying out at the toe, which is how Duck got his nickname.

Moreira heard Duck bragging about his quickness and his sharp eye in a knife fight and, although the subject appealed to him, he decided to go outside and bed down immediately. It was best to avoid trouble. Getting food for himself and his animals, he waved good night to the assembled gauchos.

"Why don't you have a drink, friend?" asked Duck, unhappy to see the newcomer not join his audience.

Moreira thanked him but politely excused himself because he had to get started early tomorrow, and Duck finished his story in disappointment. When it was done, Duck turned the conversation to the newcomer, who was presumably now asleep. All agreed that they had never seen a finer stallion than the dappled bay, with its silver-trimmed saddle and bridle. Someone said that the fellow had sold a small herd of horses earlier that afternoon, Indian horses without brands, and Duck reckoned that the newcomer must be some kind of bandit. Someone else said, "No, for God's sake, hush, that's Juan Moreira," and he told what he had heard about how two contingents of mounted police had tried to arrest Moreira, on two separate occasions, and barely survived to tell the tale. Duck, who was very drunk, reckoned he didn't care who it was, because he could take a man's measure just by looking at him. And he could tell that this newcomer was a coward.

And with that, he marched out the door, with several of his friends behind him trying to dissuade him.

Outside in the darkness, Moreira had heard the highpoints of the drunken conversation. He continued to lie quietly facedown on his poncho, but around his hand he had rolled the wide leather strip of his horsewhip, with its heavy silver handle. He was tired of getting his knife bloody.

Duck went to where Moreira lay and said:

"They've told me you're pretty good, my friend. So I want to see if the stories are true, or if they're a pack of lies!"

Moreira looked up at him sleepily and yawned, as if not understanding.

"Get up, friend," explained Duck, drawing his facón and putting the point of it on Moreira's back for a moment, "because a man that thinks he's tough has to be ready to put up or shut up, whenever, wherever, see?"

"How about *sober* up?" replied Moreira. "You go sober up, because you don't even know what you're saying, and tomorrow we'll talk about it, how about?"

"Up *yours!*" shouted the drunk Duck. "Speaking of which, time to open you a new one!"

Moreira had started to rise in the darkness as soon as he heard Duck start to shout, and when Duck finished shouting, his intended victim was no longer lying down under the point of his knife. Duck searched the ground in vain and Moreira swung his heavy silver whip handle by the leather strap onto Duck's head, sitting him down on the ground like a sack of potatoes.

Duck's friends hustled him inside, but his skull was in pieces. A man who was there that night has described the wound to me as a depression eight centimeters long, in which bits of skull and scalp were mixed with bits of brain matter. Duck's friends put a rag soaked in cane liquor on his head and hoped for the best, but by morning he was a dead Duck.

When Moreira got up the next morning—he slept right where he was lying when Duck attacked him—he shared the mate gourd with Duck's friends, who found nothing to reproach in his behavior. Then, after examining his saddle, bridle, and weapons with special care, he took the road to Matanzas.

xviii

W hat powerful emotion seized his heart when he approached his old neighborhood! How the sweet air of home filled his lungs!

There was Vicenta's father's house, where he had met and fallen in love with her, linking his existence to hers for all eternity. There was his little house, where they had lived together as newlyweds, now abandoned, without any sign whatsoever of human occupation. Happy images from the past came flooding back—his wife, his son, the way that the whole neighborhood had liked and respected him. Moreira sank into an abyss of meditation from which he emerged, minutes later with a glint of annihilation in his eye. He contemplated the awful present, with everything lost, his beloved Vicenta in the arms of another man, his son probably calling that man "father."

There are situations in life that cannot be evaluated by a person who has not experienced them, feelings of heartbreak that constitute a species of insanity, feelings that are only erased by death. The feelings that coursed through Juan Moreira during his homecoming to Matanzas fall into that category, for he had suffered the supreme insult, the worst affront that any man can endure, which must be kept in mind when judging his actions.

Moreira found a place to conceal himself nearby and gazed at his home somberly, in silence, thirsting for revenge and contemplating where to strike first. What was the worst offense that had been done to him? Mentally, he ranked them and planned to stab each offender a certain number of times, according to the severity of his offense. He gazed for hours, as darkness fell, hardly moving, poised to strike, like a wild beast stalking its prey or a murderer calculating exactly where in the back to stab his victim. He remained still, his expression unaltered, for more hours, until he thought it late enough. Now his victims would be asleep.

Then he rode straight to the house of his compadre Giménez without being seen by anyone. Little did the occupants of the house suspect that an avenging angel hovered outside, a few feet away.

Giménez had clearly worried much about Moreira since the occasion of Julián's visit, because he was well prepared. Now he slept every night with a saddled horse just outside his window and two large, fierce watchdogs in the bedroom. Moreira's normally cool judgment was addled by his monomaniacal focus on vengeance, apparently. He neglected to do enough reconnaissance, and so he did not discover his compadre's escape horse or detect the presence of the watchdogs.

Setting foot to earth outside the house, he tiptoed to the door and put his ear to it. No matter how silently Moreira moved, however, the watchdogs heard him and began to growl.

Inside, Giménez leapt out of bed and dressed rapidly as the dogs rushed to the door, scratching it with their powerful paws and barking thunderously. Vicenta awoke with a start and her half-dressed bedmate softly covered her mouth with his hand to say "be quiet." Then he crossed the room to stand near the window, ready to jump through it and onto his horse if Moreira came through the flimsy door.

Outside, Moreira seemed for once indecisive in action. When the dogs started jumping against the door, his first impulse was to fire his trabucos through it, but he had stopped with the thought that so much flying metal might injure his son. As he put his trabucos back in his belt, Moreira's hand shook. He still did not know what to do, yet he was losing the advantage of surprise completely.

Drawing his facón, he took a few steps and kicked down the door. Out came the enormous dogs to fulfill their function, which was to slow Moreira down while Giménez made his escape out the window. In seconds, the treacherous compadre had untied his horse and galloped away.

Meanwhile, the dogs leapt at Moreira with snapping jaws, and if he stopped defending himself from them for a single second, they would tear him apart. He found himself unable to pursue his most hated enemy, simply because he could not get away.

"My revenge, my revenge," howled the gaucho, killing one of the dogs with a series of powerful kicks.

At the sound of Moreira's voice, a terrible scream sounded in the pitch blackness of the room. It was the sort of scream that one imagines hearing from the patients of an insane asylum, and when Moreira heard it, he suddenly froze in the darkness, not reacting when the surviving dog bit his leg. Vicenta had recognized his voice, and believing him to be dead, she thought he was a ghost. In this, readers, she was no more credulous than most of the ignorant common folk of the countryside, who believe in all manner of spirits and signs.

"It's the spirit of my Juan!" exclaimed the poor woman, truly terrified. "He can't find peace!"

Clutching little Juan to her breast, she began to say every prayer that she knew as quickly as possible.

Moreira was profoundly moved by the sound of the voice that he had remembered so often and had not heard in so long. He held out his left arm, wrapped in his poncho, and when the second dog sank its teeth into the wool, Moreira slipped his facón into its heart almost absent-mindedly. Immediately, he released the knife handle, put his hands to his face, and began to sob.

When Vicenta heard Moreira sobbing, she found a box of matches beside the bed and lit one. And there he was, a breathing flesh-and-blood Juan Moreira, whom she had thought dead. In an instant, she understood how she had offended him, although unintentionally, and imagined, all too easily, the living hell that he had endured on her account. The expression of her youthful face passed from terror to agony, her mouth moved but pronounced no words, and her eyes stared vacantly.

The match burned away, singeing her fingers before she reacted by dropping it. After a moment, it was Moreira's turn to strike a match. Looking around the room, he saw a candle stuck in the neck of a bottle on the table and lit it.

Vicenta continued to stare uncomprehendingly, as if she'd suddenly gone mad. Moreira contemplated her for a moment, before the sound of a child softly crying attracted his eyes to the place where his beloved son lay unharmed, though frightened by the barking and loud voices.

Moreira took his son in his arms, kissing him tenderly but as fervently as if wanting to suck the blood right out of him. Then he held the child at arm's length and examined him with an almost maternal thoroughness. And finally, he started hugging and kissing him again, trying to make up in an instant for the longing of many months. The little boy recognized his father instantly, it seemed, returning his affection with equal fervor and asking in his charming, childish way where Moreira had been so long.

Vicenta seemed not to see what was happening in front of her and, after a few minutes, Moreira tucked little Juan in bed and turned to his wife. He looked at her without even a touch of rancor, and the idea of killing her or hurting her in any way never crossed his mind. He felt truly sorry for all that she had suffered without deserving it.

"Vicenta," the gaucho said solemnly, "come here. Come closer because I haven't come here to hurt you, because I forgive what you've done."

Vicenta's expressionless face began to take on an expression, and her eyes, a sudden intensity as she looked first at her husband and then at her son. Then she burst into tears, tears that flowed copiously for many minutes thereafter.

"Is it really you?" she sobbed. "You're not dead? They all lied to me?" She covered her face with her hands in shame.

Moreira's cheeks were red, as well, and he wanted suddenly to leave. Reaching down, he pulled his knife out of the second dog.

"Kill me quickly," whimpered Vicenta, thinking that he was about to execute her for disloyalty.

"God keep me from such a thing," said Moreira, sheathing his blade. "You don't deserve it, and anyway, our son needs you, because I can't take him with me. Besides, once I get my revenge, I'll truly have nothing to live for, and then I won't last long. Farewell, Vicenta, farewell forever."

Going over to the bed, the gaucho stamped a loud kiss on the forehead of his son and, covering his face with his hand, he started to leave the house when Vicenta threw herself on the floor in his path and grabbed him around the legs.

"Kill me, then, before you go," she cried, "kill me like a dog because I've dishonored and offended and disappointed you."

"Never," said Juan Moreira. "Who would take care of *him* then? Now let go of me because I have to go!"

"Juancito!" called Vicenta to the little boy, "ask your father not to go!"

Moreira blew a kiss to his son and threw himself out the door. In a flash, he was mounted and galloping away, but not fast enough to outrun the sound of Vicenta and Juancito calling him desperately. The sound wafted to him cruelly on the cool night air.

Hell in his heart, a volcano in his head, Moreira galloped toward the office of the Justice of the Peace, where he leapt from his horse and pounded on the heavy door with the silver handle of his horsewhip.

"Who's there?" inquired the voice of a soldier annoyed at being awakened.

"Juan Moreira, who wants to die in a fair fight," replied our hero. "Come out and fight, all of you who aren't cowards!"

"Your mother knows Juan Moreira, maybe," railed the voice inside the door. "Go sleep it off, why don't you?"

Moreira insisted that if the police didn't come out and fight, he would set fire to the building. Inside, the police were becoming convinced that he really was who he said.

"Come back tomorrow," said the police sergeant from behind the door. "The Justice of the Peace has gone home and left orders not to open the door to anyone."

In frustration and disgust, Moreira mounted and rode through the streets of Matanzas shouting imprecations at the townspeople who opened their shutters to see what the fuss was about. He was so desperate to fight someone, anyone, that he dismounted at all the pulperías he passed and pounded on their doors, too, shouting that it was Juan Moreira and to open up. No response.

So he galloped out of town, back the way that he had come, toward the frontier town of El Veinticinco de Mayo. Gradually he calmed down, reflecting that he did not want to die before getting his revenge. He traveled most of the next day, stopping finally at a pulpería where he was fairly well known and greeted warmly.

Soon he was in party mode, drinking and telling stories about life among the Indians. He was ready to fight the army and the Buenos

Aires police at the very least, because the cops of these two-bit pampa towns hardly made him break a sweat. It was about two o'clock in the morning when Moreira paid everyone's bill, "with Indian money," as he said, and headed on toward his destination, and it was an hour after dawn when he got to the last pulpería before El Veinticinco de Mayo.

There he caught up on the local news. The death of Duck a few days earlier had exposed the identity of Moreira, and the local police had mobilized to find him. They were led by a veteran sergeant of fame for his bravery and devotion, the kind of adversary that Moreira didn't like because he found it distasteful to kill such a man.

So our hero decided to celebrate, all drinks were on him, and he picked up the guitar that one finds in any pulpería and "scrubbed off" a dance tune or three. The party really got going then. Virtually everyone had a few and danced to Moreira's guitar, and by siesta time, when half of the partiers were already unconscious, Moreira was still playing, horse races were planned, and it looked like it would be a three-day affair.

The party was interrupted by the police attempt to capture Moreira, which failed just as completely as the reader can imagine. The brave sergeant played his part well, but as soon as Moreira's trabucos began to wreak havoc among the soldiers, they turned tail and ran. Moreira cut the sergeant's forehead, his favorite way of defeating without killing, but the man continued to swing his sword blindly. Moreira stabbed the sergeant's horse and also his right arm, whereupon, instead of turning his horse and fleeing, the man released the reins and passed his sword to his left hand. Moreira grabbed the sword from the sergeant's hand just as his horse went down, saying he didn't know how to kill a brave man, *carajo*! Moreira carefully bandaged the sergeant's wound after washing it with cane liquor and then watched over the wounded man until the next morning.

In spite of setbacks, Moreira's legend continued to grow.

xix

Now Juan Moreira became an outlaw in earnest, ranging over a broad area of countryside, including the localities of Cañuelas,

Saladillo, Lobos, Salto, and Las Heras, with Navarro as his chief center of operations. He had the police of these places completely under his spell. Although they skirmished with him occasionally, rarely did they stand and fight after his first volley with the trabucos. A pulpería-cum-brothel named La Estrella became the outlaw's legendary hangout, where he partied for two or three days at a time unmolested by the authorities. In fact, people said that these were the safest gatherings around, because Moreira wouldn't allow trouble when he was enjoying himself.

Moreira's main focus was actually the railroad station in Lobos. Several stagecoach lines brought passengers to take the train in Lobos, and Moreira was in the habit of going out to stop the stagecoaches on the highway, hoping he'd find his compadre on one and have his revenge. The passengers came armed to the teeth to their encounter with the famous outlaw, but when Moreira stepped out into the road to stop the stage and had the passengers get out, they were normally too frightened to do anything but tremble as he carefully examined the interior of the coach. When he had satisfied himself that his enemy was not within, Moreira let the coach continue without harming any passenger in the least. They even kept all their money.

One day, a friend of Moreira's informed him that the man he hated so much had bought a train ticket from Lobos to Buenos Aires. As it happened, on the same day, a party of mounted police went out to look for the famous outlaw, but Moreira gave that circumstance no importance whatsoever. He waited for the stagecoach at a pulpería on its route.

Just at noon, the stagecoach appeared in the distance, approaching rapidly. It was a large one, with eight passengers and a crew of seven, some of whom rode alongside. One of the passengers was Giménez, who had bought a modern Remington repeating rifle for the occasion of his trip to Buenos Aires.

Seeing that the party did not intend to stop at the pulpería, Moreira stepped into the road, commanding the stagecoach to stop.

"Friend Moreira," protested the driver, slowing but not stopping, "we'll miss the train if we stop."

Moreira pulled a heavy trabuco from his tirador, and the stagecoach halted suddenly, as if reaching the end of a steel tether. The outlaw strode to the window of the passenger compartment.

As usual, the heavily armed passengers declined to put up a fight at all. Giménez, in particular, had dropped his new Remington and gotten face down on the floor of the passenger compartment, begging the others to cover him up with baggage. It seemed a hopeless stratagem, for he was not the only passenger who had recognized and responded to Moreira's voice. Vicenta and little Juan had, as well. Vicenta covered her face with her hands and began to wail, while in her arms little Juan extended his arms toward Moreira, babbling his absolute delight.

Moreira leaned in the window and froze, transfixed by the sight of his son, whom he ogled with an expression of indescribable tenderness, forgetting absolutely everything else. After a moment, he reached in avidly to rumple the boy's hair and give him a thousand caresses. The passengers watched in wonder and gradually relaxed as Juancito begged his papá in the most charming way to take him for a ride, a request that Moreira appeared unable to refuse, until, suddenly, he heard Cacique's bark, let go of the boy, pulled out his other trabuco, and turned toward the road to face a new threat. The look of supreme tenderness vanished from his eye, replaced by one of fury and mayhem.

The gaucho sprinted to where his horse stood and saw ten or twelve mounted police coming toward him at a gallop. They had seen his horse first and hoped, by taking it, to cut off his escape. They had gotten fairly close, with Moreira lost in the contemplation of his son, not hearing Cacique's bark at first.

The police squad slowed to a trot and approached with caution. They had "kill on sight" orders for Moreira and no longer tried to arrest him. Seeing his chance, the stagecoach driver whipped his horses and the vehicle pulled away. Moreira cursed; there went his revenge again! He resolved to make short work of the soldiers and then catch up with the stagecoach.

The soldiers stopped. They had been especially equipped with carbines for the task of killing Juan Moreira, but as they had not been effectively trained to use them, all their bullets went wide of the target. Moreira simply stood and laughed as they fired at him, not even bothering to take cover. Then he leveled his trabucos, killed or wounded several of the soldiers, and reloaded before the smoke cleared.

The remaining nine or ten soldiers were desperately trying to spur their military-issue nags into a charge when the smoke cleared, and Moreira let them come in something like slow motion. Boom went the trabucos, again, and the police had had enough, bolting away in a panic, leaving three of their number dead on the field.

Moreira thrust his trabucos into his tirador, leapt onto his horse, and for the first time ever, he pursued the fleeing soldiers, who lived in terror of his name. These were no better nor worse than any others, but they had committed an unforgiveable sin, interrupting his paternal idyll and preventing him, once again, from avenging himself on that dog Giménez. The fleeing riders fanned out, and Moreira chose one to follow, pulled out one of his double-barreled pistols, doubled his reins in one fist, and put his sharp spurs hard into the flanks of the dappled bay horse, which was off like a shot.

After three or four minutes, Moreira had closed the distance between him and the doomed soldier to a couple of lengths. The desperate man turned to fire a last shot at Moreira, missed, of course, and then pulled his saber and swung at Moreira, once. That's all he had time for. It was scarcely the kind of fight that makes a good story. The soldier defended himself bravely, but Moreira was not in a mood for magnanimity, nor did he have time for it. He leveled his pistol and, as he was only a few feet away and doesn't miss what he shoots at, more or less blew the soldier's head off with both barrels.

Somewhat mollified, the outlaw wheeled the dappled bay and galloped back the way that he had come, past the pulpería, down the road that the stagecoach would have taken to the train station, but it was no use, he had lost too much time fighting the police and then pursuing them. After five miles he halted to scan the horizon carefully and, seeing nothing, regretfully gave up.

Moreira returned to the pulpería and threw a bucket of water on the back of his dappled bay horse. He ordered sangría for his own thirst and went out to lie down near his horse. He spent the rest of the day there, and the customers of the pulpería heard him weep and repeat his son's name many times.

They say that around nightfall he went out to stop another stagecoach on its way to the Lobos railroad station, although it isn't clear why. Or rather, he did say that "nobody else passes today, because those that shouldn't have, already did," so perhaps it was simply pique. In any case, when one of the passengers apparently spoke to him without hostility or grand airs, saying, "Friend Moreira, I'll lose a lot of money if I miss the train to Buenos Aires," he apparently relented and let them through, showing once again what I have explained a thousand times. Moreira was not born a criminal, although he did gradually become one. His instincts were noble, however, as he always showed when people were good to him.

We can see that yet again in what occurred next, in Navarro, where Moreira's old friend Marañón, the gentleman whose life he had saved on a dark street, had become Justice of the Peace there. Moreira went straight to the crowded pulpería of Olazo near the center of town, the place where he had fought Leguizamón, and started buying drinks.

For the next couple of hours, he was in his element, telling stories about life among the Indians.

Then he paid everyone's bill, said he'd like to take a turn around the town square, and mounted to go down the block toward the office of the Justice of the Peace. Half the customers of Olazo followed him, expecting that there would be something to see. Everybody knew that all the police for miles around had standing orders to kill Moreira on sight.

Moreira stopped at the door of the Justice of the Peace's office, looked at the soldier who stood guard there, pulled out both trabucos, and checked if they were loaded correctly.

"Aren't the other police on duty?" he asked, putting his trabucos back in his tirador. "Go tell the sergeant that Juan Moreira's here to fight."

The guard entered, closed the door, and didn't come back. Eventually, Moreira got down and pounded on the door with the handle of his horsewhip. Finally, the door opened, and the police sergeant appeared to speak in a stage whisper.

"Go away, please, don Juan," implored the sergeant. "No one here wants to fight you, and if Doctor Marañón gets back and finds out you were here, there'll be problems for sure."

When he learned that Marañón was Justice of the Peace in Navarro, the gaucho changed his attitude instantly and took his leave, saying that "he would not tangle with the law in Navarro" as long as his friend was the judge there.

Moreira went to spend the night at the house of acquaintances on the edge of town, and it was about eight o'clock that evening when Cacique announced the arrival, hat in hand, of the police sergeant from that afternoon. He had a message for Moreira from the Justice of the Peace, inviting him to talk.

This may seem privileged information, and of course, the idea that a judge would call a man like Juan Moreira to his house for a private conversation may strike some as inappropriate. It is not my intention to offend a distinguished gentleman whose immaculate reputation speaks for itself, and I apologize should any offense be taken. In my eyes, Marañón's treatment of Moreira constitutes the highest guarantee of the judge's moral caliber.

The judge renewed his earlier offer to help our hero make a new start in some distant province, yet Moreira steadfastly rejected the idea. He spoke in the darkest, most fatalistic terms about simply wanting a good death, now—a death worthy of his legend.

"I'll need you not to do it here," said Marañón, "because I'll resign as judge rather than fight you."

"Oh, I'll leave, sir, don't worry," said the gaucho, "tonight, in fact. But if you want to be the man who captured Juan Moreira, if that's good for you, I mean, well you can just say the word, and I'll come to your house and tie myself up."

"That's crazy," said Marañón. "Just don't stay in Navarro, and good luck."

"Good-bye, boss!" said the gaucho fervently as he took Marañón's hand in two of his own.

Again the judge urged Moreira to reconsider. Why, he'd even promise to deliver Juancito to him in that distant province of new beginnings!

Two tears rolled down our hero's cheek, but he made no further answer. His mind was made up. Half an hour later, he rode out of town, taking the direction of Salto.

XX

Shortly after the events of the previous chapter, a stranger appeared in the locality of Salto, Juan Blanco by name.

Blanco's clothing was a mix of city and countryside, one could say, made of the very finest materials. Black boots with silver spurs inlaid with gold, and billowing out of the boot tops, black cashmere *bombacha* trousers instead of the old-fashioned chiripá worn by Juan Moreira. Blanco in fact looked very much like Moreira, with the same blue jacket and broad-brimmed hat, although his hair had been cut and his beard shaved except for the chin. His tirador was different, the new one so densely studded with silver coins that the leather underneath was hardly visible, but stuffed into it was a familiar arsenal: two trabucos and two double-barreled pistols. Thrust under his tirador at the small of his back, the gaucho incognito carried a celebrated two-foot-long facón in a silver sheath.

Blanco cut a dazzling figure in Salto. He rode into town on a dappled bay stallion that all the men envied, his hat tipped back on the nape of his neck so that all the women could get a good look at his handsome face. He rode right up to the office of the Justice of the Peace, declared that he had recently sold significant property elsewhere and was coming to live in Salto, and asked to join the local National Guard unit. The military commander of Salto was thrilled to write down his name.

Juan Blanco's reputation had preceded him. Although no one knew who he was, exactly, everyone knew, apparently, that the police had failed many times to arrest him and that he was almost invincible one-on-one. They knew he liked music, because he showed up without an invitation at all the dances in town, without anyone's daring to challenge him, either—the men, that is, because none of the women minded Blanco's handsome, if uninvited, presence in the least. On the contrary, he loved to dance and never stepped on their feet.

The incident that defined Blanco's legend in Salto occurred at a wake, the kind where the mourners celebrate the life of the deceased by tying one on and dancing till dawn. Among the mourners that night, in addition to Blanco, was an Assistant Justice whom the women of Salto also liked a lot. Someone pointed out the prettiest country girl there as the Assistant Justice's current interest. So Blanco went straight to ask her to dance, and dance they did. She was all over him after a while but always watching the lawman out of the corner of her eye, and the lawman naturally got disgruntled after a while, which she could easily detect, and then she enjoyed dancing with the gallant, well-dressed stranger even more.

Finally, Blanco let the girl sit down, just as the accordion and guitar launched into a polka, and immediately the Assistant Justice appeared by her chair with his hand extended, inviting her to dance. She was about to get up but happened to glance at Blanco, who indicated with a gesture that she should remain seated, which she did. The fury that had been accumulating inside the lawman all evening finally exploded into shouting.

"My friend, this women belongs to someone, and that someone is me, so take this as a warning!"

"A warning!" laughed Blanco. "Why, you almost sound like an Assistant Justice!"

This particular Assistant Justice had a serious reputation, but given that the representatives of our legal system are so unanimously hated in the interior of the Republic, it is not surprising that the crowd smiled at Blanco's joke and seemed to take his side. Partly, they liked what they knew of him, and partly, they wanted to see the lawman taken down a notch, whoever did it. The Assistant Justice of the Peace puffed himself up to full size. In front of all these people, he was deter-mined to impose respect, and ready to fight for it, too.

"The dignity of my office does not permit me to accept your attempts at humor," he said. "Get out of here, or you'll sleep with your head in the stocks."

Blanco looked back at the furious lawman with a grin, then turned to the many faces that contemplated this little drama and looked at them, then laughed so frankly, whimsically, and uproariously, that everyone in the room ended up laughing along with him—everyone, that is, except the lawman.

This lawman, though, was of the modern variety who carry a revolver. He drew his and put the muzzle on Blanco's forehead, which was possible only because the gaucho did not withdraw his head even slightly.

"Get out of here," he repeated, "or you're under arrest."

The crowd shuddered. They didn't much like this Assistant Justice, but they knew him not to make idle threats. They watched more avidly than ever, but they began to pull back, too.

Blanco, who had been seated, stopped chuckling, rose slowly, and stepped away, keeping his eyes on the gun.

"I've sworn not to kill except in self-defense," said the gaucho, "but don't push me. I think that *you're* the one who needs to leave. Even though you're a lawman, I'll have mercy on you this time."

The Assistant Justice stomped the floorboards with his boot heel and again placed the barrel of his revolver against Blanco's forehead.

"Let's go, then!" he commanded. "Move before I pop this mate gourd and spill its contents all over the place."

This was one of those cases in which Juan Moreira, because that's of course who it really was, moved more quickly than the eye could follow. The spectators only saw the result of the action, which was that the mysterious stranger, Juan Blanco, had brought his fist up under the lawman's jaw with enough power to lift him off his feet and send him flying through the air like a sack of potatoes to land in front of the accordion player, where he lay still.

Blanco picked up the revolver and threw it out the door, pulled the unconscious lawman off the dance floor, then clapped his hands.

"Come on, people, let's dance," he said gaily, and to the band, "Something up-tempo, come on!"

The accordion and guitar struck up a serviceable tune, Blanco extended his hand to the girl who all the fuss was about, and away they went, but not for long. The lawman recovered his senses, calculated the depth of his public humiliation, and broke up the dance before the first song could conclude.

As people rushed out of the way, the lawman came at Blanco, knife in hand. Blanco pulled out his riding whip, which he'd been carrying rolled up and tucked under his gleaming tirador. Holding the leather portion, he swung its heavy silver handle like a mace, making it hum through the air. The whirling weight crashed into the lawman's wrist before he could get close to Blanco, knocking the knife out of his hand. Then Blanco took his whip by the handle, and horse-whipped the cowering Assistant Justice in front of everybody, leaving him bloody and humiliated.

The fame of Juan Blanco reached its zenith at that moment.

Still, it wasn't the best thing for the party, and people began to leave. Blanco said good-bye to his dance partner and told the bereaved family that he was sorry for their loss. He regretted that there had been a minor scuffle, which he had tried to avoid. The partiers getting on their horses to go home were amused to find a little dog walking back and forth on the saddle of the dappled bay stallion.

Blanco waved good-bye and, because it was still rather early, headed for the center of the town of Salto.

The story of the Assistant Justice's horsewhipping got to the center of town before Juan Blanco did, though. The crowd at the billiard parlor had already heard several versions of it when our hero walked in. They bought him drinks. Was it really true what he had just done? They were amazed. The man was a walking arsenal, and yet, when that lily-livered so-and-so put a gun to his head, he defended himself with his bare hands and then horsewhipped the little puke on the dance floor! Talk about style. It was possibly the most fantastic thing that had ever happened in Salto. They had only one question. Why hadn't he killed him?

"I'm not going to muck up my blade anymore with the blood of lawmen," declared Juan Blanco, who was well pleased by all the attention, "except when I want to."

"You'll have to get out of here now, though," declared his new friends.

"Why on earth?" protested Blanco. "If the police don't come looking for me in a few days, maybe I'll go looking for them!"

To say that Juan Blanco was well received in Salto would be an understatement. His new friends didn't even mind much when they caught him cheating at billiards. For him, and for them, too, cheating was sport, skill at it was admired, and winning by breaking the rules was fine as long as you didn't get caught. Besides, who was going to challenge a man like Juan Blanco?

xxi

That night, and every night, Blanco rode out of town and slept under the stars, facedown on his poncho, beside his dappled bay horse, behavior that was unlikely to establish him as a solid citizen of Salto. Was he really trying to turn over a new leaf? If so, the scene at the famous wake didn't help. It was the inexhaustible topic of conversation among all the inhabitants of the town for the better part of two days, when an even better story replaced it.

The reigning desperado among the gauchos of Salto was Rico Romero. Romero was rich, as his nickname said, and his reputation for bravery, well deserved. The rising star of Juan Blanco wounded his tough guy pride. To hear people prating on about Blanco, "a bull of a man," made Romero physically ill, and he was determined to fight the upstart at the first opportunity.

The night after the wake, Romero went early to the billiard hall and stayed all evening, hoping that Blanco would appear. Instead, for hours he endured the torment of hearing the customers sing Blanco's praises.

"He's a real man, believe me," everyone assured Romero, "fast as greased lighting, too."

"It wouldn't take much of a man to cold-cock that Assistant Justice," he carped. "And I don't care how fast he is, he'll stop moving completely when I'm finished with him."

Romero and his interlocutors looked up to see Blanco standing by their table. It was impossible that he had not heard Romero's last remark.

"Good evening, gentlemen," said Blanco.

Romero assumed that fear motivated Blanco's failure to respond to his provocation. All Salto knew Romero's reputation, and surely Blanco knew it, as well, if he was the fighter that everyone said. And of course, Romero was correct in the second part of his supposition.

Blanco well knew who he was. Yet, when Romero, alone among the men at the table, failed to acknowledge Blanco's friendly greeting, Blanco shrugged off the slight and turned to converse with a couple of gauchos who stood leaning against the bar.

Not five minutes had passed before the frustrated tough guy began making loud, aggressive comments to the men seated at the table, turning his head toward Blanco at a strategic moment in each declamation to indicate a good example of what he disparaged. Some fools wanted to keep their reputation without fighting, it seems. They get as meek as a lamb or roll up in a ball like a little armadillo when someone gives them a poke.

The provocations were not lost on Blanco, but still he resisted becoming involved in another fight and, instead, invited his friends at the bar to play billiards. He must have been aware that his stock with the masculine public of Salto had plummeted 50 percent because of his mild-mannered acceptance of Rico Romero's abuse. He wanted to do the right thing.

Romero turned in his chair to face the billiard table and drank another glass of gin as he watched the game. The men whom Blanco had invited to play were practiced pool sharks, and yet he found a way to win, calling Lady Luck invisibly to his side with a sleight of hand that none of my sources can specify. If the other players saw him cheat, they didn't say so, nor would we expect them to. After a while, tired of Blanco's way of winning, the other players gradually gave up.

When the last one left and Blanco stood alone by the billiard table, rolling the ivory balls around with his hand, his lurking enemy finally spoke.

"I'll play you for a hundred pesos and drinks for everybody here," said Rico Romero, rising and walking to the billiard table.

Blanco pulled a stack of silver coins from his tirador and placed his bet on the table. The rich gaucho produced a one-hundred-peso note and put it beside Blanco's coins, saying:

"One thing, though: I can't stand a cheater. Try it, and I'll split you in half."

Blanco's new peaceful demeanor seemed imperturbable, his smile, as eternal as if painted on his face. He arranged the balls on the billiard table to begin the game as all the other customers took positions of spectatorship. One way or another, this would be worth seeing.

For the first ten minutes or so, there were billiards worth seeing, because Romero was quite a good player in spite of the generous amount of gin he'd drunk waiting for Blanco all evening. Nor did the actions of either player suggest what was about to happen.

Then Blanco simply could not resist his usual cheating. How could he? It was just too amusing to get away with, but Romero saw it. Picking up a billiard ball, he threw it at Blanco with all his might from across the table. The ball hit Blanco's chest with a loud thump, knocking the air out of him.

Blanco raised his hand to his chest and swore. Romero jumped on the table and swung his billiard cue at Blanco, who ducked and dodged until Romero jumped down.

Neither man had drawn a blade at this point, although both carried one. The witnesses agree on this point. Blanco, as we know, was trying to turn over a new leaf, but Romero wasn't, and besides, he was a good bit shorter than Blanco—perhaps the reason that he'd climbed on the table.

He was heavier, though, and seeing Blanco still unarmed, Romero tackled him around the waist, meaning to throw him to the floor where height would be no advantage. Blanco was heavier than he looked, however. He didn't topple so easily, and meanwhile Romero's facón, still in its sheath at the small of his back, was within easy reach of Blanco's hand. Blanco grabbed it.

At that moment, he could easily have cut the rich tough guy's throat, but instead, still playing the part of Juan Blanco, he simply used the heavy pommel of the facón as a hammer to soften up the base of Romero's skull. Indeed, he was altogether too gentle, because, while Romero dropped to the floor, he did not stay still. Instead, he slithered away like a fat worm, sprang to his feet, and reached for his facón, which was, of course, not there.

"A knife!" shouted Romero, and he tried to wrench one away from a nearby spectator who, as he was not expecting the town's reigning tough guy to emerge victorious, declined to cooperate. Blanco's stock had recovered, it seems, as quickly as it had declined. Full of self-confidence, he threw Romero's knife back to him, drew his own, and wrapped his poncho around his left arm.

Romero was clearly outclassed. With his shorter arms, he couldn't get close enough to Blanco to wet his blade in the other man's blood. He had a tendency to lower his head and charge like a bull in a bullfight, and on one such pass, Blanco thwacked him on the back of his sore head with the flat of his blade.

Aware that he would probably not be alive much longer, Romero planned and executed his final ploy. His enemy would have to drop his guard and lose focus for a moment, then he could get inside those longer arms and spill his guts on the floor!

Taking a billiard ball from the table, Romero threw it at Blanco and charged right behind it, hoping that his adversary would flinch and dodge, giving Romero the opening that he needed so badly.

But Blanco did not flinch or dodge. Instead, he took the blow of the billiard ball squarely in the chest and watched Romero come lumbering at him behind it with everything he had. So Romero found no opening when he got within reach of Blanco's facón, but it was too late to stop.

Aiming carefully between the third and fourth ribs, which is the sort of thing that a knife-fighter learns to calculate after a while, Blanco slipped the long blade into the oncoming Romero and held it firm while the enraged and panting loser more or less dove onto it. Romero lived just long enough to realize that he was impaling himself on Blanco's blade, straight through his heart, in fact, but not long enough to diminish the impulse that drove him forward. So powerful was that impulse that Blanco had to put a knee on the corpse's chest to get his facón out of it because the point had penetrated, as subsequent examination of the blade indicated, nearly half an inch into a vertebra.

Blanco casually wiped his knife blade on what was left of Rico Romero and put it back in its silver sheath as the patrons of the billiard parlor watched intently. Blanco ordered a round of drinks for the house, downed his in a single gulp, paid for everything, and walked out of the billiard parlor without anything more being said.

Outside, he looked up and down the street. It was only nine o'clock in the evening, still early. Scooping Cacique out of the way, he mounted and rode toward the center of town, toward the office of the Justice of the Peace. He stopped one block short of it, however, when he saw a barber shop open.

The barber himself tells the story as follows. The well-dressed stranger had walked in and asked for a trim of his stylishly short hair and beard. Just as the barber began to pass his straight razor blade along the customer's cheek, down toward his throat, the man spoke.

"Tell me, friend," he inquired, "if Juan Moreira walked in and asked for a shave, just the way that I've done today, what would you do?"

"Shave him," shrugged the barber, "because I don't want trouble."

"What if he then refused to pay?" laughed the customer.

"Then he wouldn't pay, because I don't want trouble. But they say he's a good man, forced into a life of crime," said the barber.

And for his kind words, the stranger gave him a fifty-peso bill and refused to accept change.

"Keep it," he had said, "as a memento of Juan Moreira."

Our hero had given up the charade and wanted his own name back. He climbed on his horse, rode past the office of the Justice of the Peace, closed at that hour, took a turn around the dusty town square, and headed for the dark neighborhoods at the edge of town. The barber closed his shop right after the mysterious customer left, and within half an hour everybody in Salto had heard that Blanco was really Moreira. Mystery solved! Nobody was surprised, anymore, by the spectacle of the Assistant Justice horsewhipped on the dance floor or Rico Romero stuck like a pig in the billiard parlor ruckus.

Sure, it was Juan Moreira. Of course!

If the Salto police had already been afraid of Juan Blanco, imagine how they greeted the news. They even dared disobey the Justice of the Peace when he ordered them to arrest Moreira. Before Moreira left the town, which he did within a day or two, he actually went to the office of the Justice of the Peace and pounded on the heavy door with the handle of his horsewhip.

"It's me, Juan Moreira! Come out and fight, cowards!"

But the Justice of the Peace wasn't in, and the police contingent pretended not to be, either.

xxii

By 1873, Juan Moreira had become a kind of power unto himself on the pampa. Therefore, during that year's elections, all the parties wanted him on their side.

After leaving Salto, the gaucho went back to Navarro, where he had participated in politics before. This time, Moreira joined the party that resisted the candidacy of Avellaneda. The partisans of Avellaneda made a concerted attempt to woo Moreira to their side, all for nothing.

At one point, a distinguished gentleman whose name I will omit, founded a pro-Avellaneda political club in Navarro, and he offered Moreira fifty thousand pesos to join it. Moreira sent word that he would go to the next meeting of the pro-Avellaneda club to deliver his answer personally. The clubmen assumed that fifty thousand pesos constituted an offer that Moreira could not refuse.

When Moreira arrived at the club meeting on the appointed evening, the sounds of celebration could be heard outside the building. The members greeted him effusively. They already counted, among their hundred or so members, some of the toughest characters in Navarro, all riding around "in election mode," which is to say, armed to the teeth. With Moreira on their side, how could they lose? Moreira went straight to the club president, who sat at a table at one end of the large room, counting out the fifty thousand pesos with which he hoped to guarantee an electoral victory.

"Money can't buy my loyalty," he said to the club president in a voice loud enough to be heard by all, "and anyway, you don't have enough of it."

"You've got it wrong, friend Moreira," offered the president, thinking that his only chance lay in sweet talk. "We need your support, true enough, though. This is what we can offer you for now, but there will be much more if we win the election."

He was about to add a few words of praise for Avellaneda, but Moreira cut him off.

"Your candidate makes me sick," he spat, "and I'm no good at organizing cowards."

Then he turned to the eighty to one hundred "cowards" he'd just alluded to, addressing them directly.

"When I'm at the polls, just *try* to vote for Avellaneda, and I'll put out your eyes with a riding whip."

The men that our political parties assemble at election time are surely the most intimidating to be found in our communities, and yet Moreira insulted the pro-Avellaneda club of Salto without a single member of that exalted organization expressing the slightest objection to his face. Then he marched straight through the crowd that he had just insulted, without once looking behind him, or even to the left or right, to fend off some treacherous attack on his person.

Outside, he mounted and rode to the anti-Avellaneda club, where he had more or less taken up residence, and on the day of the election the anti-Avellaneda forces got all the votes.

Not a single man in Navarro dared step up to the ballot box and vote publicly for Avellaneda, knowing that he would be taking his life in his hands. In the locality of Lobos, they saw that Moreira's name alone defeated Avellaneda, because the gaucho did not go there at all during the electoral campaign or on voting day. The veracity of this account can be confirmed by Casimiro Villamayor, the Justice of the Peace in Lobos at the time. At first, Avellaneda seemed to be winning in Lobos, according to Villamayor, when the opposing side spread the rumor that Juan Moreira was on his way from Navarro. After that, no other votes were added to Avellaneda's candidacy, and he lost by a landslide in Lobos.

The election over, Moreira gave himself over to wine, women, and song, as they say. He arrived at some pulpería, picked up the guitar, and started parties that might continue for as much as a week, parties that the storekeepers never objected to because he always paid the whole bill.

Naturally, though, the pro-Avellaneda forces wanted vengeance, and they began to spread untrue stories of the "horrible murders" committed by the famous outlaw. Finally, provincial governor Mariano Acosta saw the need to take action, ordering the Provincial Guard to make a sweep of the countryside, eliminating hordes of vagrants and cattle rustlers as well as "the celebrated bandit" Juan Moreira, whom they were to capture and deliver to Buenos Aires to stand trial. Little did they know!

The head of the expedition was Coronel Garmendia, a capable man, as we all know. Vagrants he found aplenty, and rustlers, too, but neither hide nor hair of Juan Moreira. It seemed that the elusive gaucho had just been wherever they looked for him, but try as they might, they couldn't lay eyes on him, much less capture him.

Once Garmendia learned that Moreira was having some rowdy fun in the pulpería of Olazo, and within minutes the Provincial Guard had surrounded it and proceeded to search it thoroughly, even moving a large stack of liquor barrels to make sure that he was not hidden there. In fact, Moreira was present, as it was later revealed, in a small basement underneath Olazo's bedroom, quietly waiting, trabucos in hand, while the soldiers searched the pulpería. Lucky for them, they didn't find him.

The anecdote helps explain why our hero was so hard to find. He was that rare thing, a man simultaneously feared and liked. Nobody with any first-hand experience of Juan Moreira believed the stories of horrible murders. Yet still Moreira's enemies spread those stories, and Governor Acosta continued to worry about them—even more so, after the failure of the Garmendia expedition.

One of those "horrible murders" generated enormous press coverage and substantially influenced public opinion in Buenos Aires. This was the murder of an Italian whose throat Moreira reportedly cut to rob him of one peso's worth of bread. Practically everything that has been published about the case is an invention of Moreira's enemies, however. I have talked with many who have direct, detailed knowledge of the real events, which were as follows.

The poor Italian was murdered, not by Moreira, but by another gaucho outlaw whose biography will shortly appear in the True Crime section of this same newspaper. The murderer stopped the Italian's cart on the highway and cut his throat for the money that the poor man had in his pockets, about three hundred pesos, more or less. The murderer was sitting beside the corpse of his victim, counting the money, when Juan Moreira, who had guessed what was happening, came galloping up.

"What happened here?" demanded Moreira.

The other outlaw did not even stop counting the money.

"You can see for yourself," he said. "Another Italian gone, and a few pesos that I might as well take before somebody else does."

"Kill for money," said Moreira indignantly, "and you'll die like a pig."

The killer, whom I have been able interview at length, declares that Moreira's words made a big impression, and Moreira's horsewhip left him begging for mercy. Moreira carefully examined the Italian to make sure he was dead, put the three hundred pesos back in the dead man's pocket, and galloped away. Witnesses who saw him leaving suspected Moreira of the crime, suspicions that the true murderer happily encouraged, and soon this new round of false accusations reached the ears of Governor Acosta: JUAN MOREIRA SLAUGHTERS BAKER FOR A LOAF OF BREAD.

Such travesties could not be tolerated, according to Governor Acosta, and he communicated as much to the Justice of the Peace of Navarro, who was still, at this juncture, none other than Moreira's great friend Marañón. The provincial government had been informed (by the embittered losers of the last election) that Marañón was protecting the outlaw. Only that protection could explain his ability to commit a string of heinous crimes without being brought to justice.

A vile calumny, obviously! My readers already know, as the people of several pampas towns, including Navarro, knew, that the police trembled at the very thought of trying to arrest Juan Moreira. They would have flatly disobeyed any order to pursue him, which is why that order was not given in Navarro. Marañón drafted an extensive reply, explaining the matter, invoking the testimony of several of the most respectable citizens of Navarro and demonstrating beyond

question that the important and thriving pampean locality lacked the
necessary police assets. So unreasonable was the provincial government, however, that it pronounced itself not satisfied by these per-
suasive explanations, and it went as far as to open an investigation of
Marañón's conduct as Justice of the Peace.

This is the sad background of the next major attempt to capture
or kill Juan Moreira. Like the last attempt, it disregarded the ten-
man local police squads who had failed so spectacularly in their own
attempts and had finally refused to pursue him altogether. The new
expedition was to be composed of twenty-five of the best police of
urban Buenos Aires, handpicked for the assignment and not charged
with improving the law and order of the countryside generally, as
Garmendia's expedition had been, but simply, expressly, and exclusively
with "bringing in the bandit Juan Moreira, dead or alive." The commander of the expedition was a tough army veteran, Adolfo Cortinas.

"I'll wipe them like snotty noses," said Moreira, in his colorful
gaucho language, when he learned of the Cortinas expedition, and he
began announcing the upcoming encounter in every pulpería that he
visited. "Too bad that there aren't fifty of them," he said, when asked if
twenty-five to one weren't bad odds even for Juan Moreira, and when
warned ominously that these police were from the big city and knew
how to use their firearms, he made a terrified face, "ooooooh, I'm
soooo scared," and then laughed his famous laugh. The local police
were secretly delighted not to be involved in the expedition. Publicly,
they wished Cortinas and the city fellows luck but privately laid odds
among themselves on how many of the twenty-five would survive.
The smart money was on seventeen, counting the commander.

Moreira's informants kept him apprised of the expedition's progress
as it detrained in Lobos and made its way from there to Navarro. Calculating its arrival for suppertime, he went to the town's principal inn
and "restaurant," if one wants to give it that name, where most of the
customers sat together at a long table facing the door. Oil lamps hung
on greasy chains over the table to provide light to the windowless room.

When Moreira sat at the far end of the big table, facing the only
entrance, and, as the other customers began to get up and leave for
other tables, he put his two trabucos in his lap, covered by his poncho,
which he had taken off before sitting down. Then he ordered a bowl
of soup and a bottle of French wine "to see if he could work up some
courage," as he said with an impish smile and a wink.

Meanwhile, neither Cortinas nor any of his men had ever seen
Moreira, though they had descriptions, so, upon entering Navarro

they looked for someone able to point him out. That turned out to be surprisingly difficult. Did so-and-so know Juan Moreira? Why, of course, everybody knew him! Well then, could he point him out? No, well . . . no, not really. And if a reward were offered? No, no thanks.

The conversation was repeated over and over, until finally, Cortinas found his Judas, Carrizo by name, a "no account" sort whom Moreira had humiliated on a certain occasion that Carrizo never forgot. After that, all the little man could do was think about revenge, but since he was a coward, he couldn't find an opportunity until Cortinas offered him one.

When Cortinas and his twenty-five troops, guided by Carrizo, arrived at the inn where Moreira awaited them, the gaucho had already finished his dinner and was thinking, with disappointment, that the lawmen weren't coming after all. Too bad, he thought, because he could use the exercise.

Cortinas sent half his force to surround the building and, still guided by Carrizo, took the other half in the front door. Moreira became suddenly cheerful when he saw Carrizo appear on the threshold, signaling him with his Judas finger.

"That is your man," said Carrizo.

"You coward, you are one dead wretch!" howled Moreira.

"Surrender, Juan Moreira," intoned Cortinas, "in the name of the Metropolitan Police of Buenos Aires."

Moreira's answer was to throw the poncho in his lap at the lamp over the table, extinguishing it and plunging the room into darkness.

Next, there was a deafening roar and a blinding flash as Moreira fired both trabucos simultaneously in familiar fashion.

Then, the staggering metropolitan police who were still on their feet, stunned and heads spinning, had the impression that Moreira was flying at them over the table, facón in hand, although they couldn't see anything clearly, amid the smoke and shadows. Instinctively they dove out of the way.

Finally, they heard from the street the sound of Moreira escaping on his dappled bay horse, which Carrizo had stupidly forgotten about; then several rifle shots, as policemen stationed outside tried to bring down the fleeing gaucho; then, finally, the sound of Moreira's guffaws as all the shots missed their mark and he galloped gaily away.

It took a moment for someone to relight the lamp, revealing three men on the very bloody floor of the room: two of the twenty-five troopers from Buenos Aires, wounded by Moreira's trabucos, and the remains of Carrizo, whose head Moreira's facón had nearly separated from his body as he flew past in the darkened room.

The Cortinas expedition returned to the great city to report its failure, and the provincial government recognized that capturing Juan Moreira was not going to be easy.

xxiii

Moreira could thwart and baffle the police at will, and he had a way with Lady Luck, but she is an inconstant lover, as we know. His options were narrowing. He continued to range over a home territory that he knew well and where he had many friends, but the campaign against him was increasingly high profile and well coordinated, and he was running out of safe houses.

Not wishing to make trouble for his friend Marañón, who was Justice of the Peace in Navarro, he went back to Lobos, where his brother Inocencio had a small ranch. Inocencio Moreira is today a police officer in Lobos. Another resident of Lobos was the colorful character that everyone called Leather Man, a redoubtable gaucho tough who pretended to be Moreira's great friend. Before long, there wasn't a pulpería in Lobos without a Moreira story: he had said this, he had done that, nobody was more gaucho than he. Even now, shortly before his death, Moreira was still the outlaw who never started a fight, but once in one, always fought fair. More and more, though, Moreira's presence indicated the possibility of a "shoot-out."

One evening the gaucho appeared at a private dance on the outskirts of Lobos, invited by the man who lived there, one of his many friends. The sight of Moreira with his two trabucos and facón at his waist visibly cooled the enthusiasm of the dancing couples at first, and, noticing as much, the gaucho remained in the doorway watching the dance without entering for several minutes. Gradually, the party spirit recovered, but Moreira was not in a happy mood.

He went to the room where there was a table with refreshments, which was a bedroom. The room filled with guests between dance numbers but was abandoned at the moment. Moreira sat on the edge of the bed, lost in meditation, when in walked Manuel Caminos, then military commander of the Lobos district, and more recently, distinguished Justice of the Peace of that prosperous and progressive locality.

Caminos was visibly surprised to find the "notorious" Juan Moreira at the party, but the outlaw spoke without hesitation, and the conversation that followed will be instructive to anyone who still wants to imagine Moreira as a crude and savage criminal. It has been given to me verbatim by Judge Caminos himself.

"Excuse me, sir," said the gaucho, "if my presence in this house offends you. I'll leave, but before I do, I have a small favor to ask of you."

And he went on to explain that, as he lived without fixed domicile, he did not have a current National Guard registration, and could Caminos do him the favor of issuing one? Judge Caminos, let me say, is kindly by nature but scrupulously honest in the execution of the responsibilities of public office.

"By no means can I fulfill your request," said the gentleman. "Rightly or wrongly, you are wanted by the law. Whatever my personal criterion in the matter, I cannot, *ipso facto*, provide the documentation that you solicit."

Caminos expected that he would have to pay dearly for this expression of administrative rectitude, but the famous outlaw made no aggressive gesture at all. Instead, he continued to sit quietly on the edge of the bed and hung his head, for a moment, before replying.

"Please," he said, finally raising his head, "I will leave Lobos immediately after I get the registration and promise never to reveal who issued it."

"I simply cannot," insisted the Caminos. "To do so would be to betray the nation's confidence, something that I will never, ever, do. Ask no more, for you are wasting your time, I assure you."

After Caminos left the room, Moreira sat for another few minutes, nodding his head slowly, as if approving the conduct of the honorable military commander. Finally, reflecting that no one had entered the room with the refreshment table between dances, he went out and sat down beside the accordion and guitar players. One can only imagine his frustration.

And yet, when a drunk gaucho started to pepper him with provocative comments, rising gradually in intensity, Moreira pretended not to notice for a long time. When the drunk pulled out a knife and staggered in Moreira's direction, he took off his poncho and threw it on top of the man, who couldn't find his way out of it and finally fell over.

Moreira left, laughing mirthlessly, and rode to La Estrella, which was among his favorite hangouts, in part, because there were "working" women there, and the establishment was open all night. There he encountered a friend named Eulogio Varela, who, on a certain occasion years earlier, before Moreira became an outlaw, had kindly lent him a horse that he needed to get from Chivilcoy to Matanzas.

The two embraced as friends, but Varela was now captain of the Lobos police force, and he begged Moreira to leave the area, because the next time that their paths crossed, it would be as lawman and outlaw.

"I am in your debt for past kindness," said the outlaw, "and so I'll leave Lobos as you say. There's too much blood on my hands, as it is."

Moreira went to the house of his brother Inocencio, whom he thought he might never see again, and stayed there three days before taking the road to Navarro. The Justice of the Peace had threatened Inocencio with prosecution unless he alerted the authorities when his brother came to visit, but of course he declined to betray his own flesh and blood. In punishment, Inocencio Moreira was conscripted into the army and sent to the frontier for two years.

Here is a lovely topic for the investigative reporting of *El Nacional*, a publication that has shown itself to be always eager to defend the iniquitous judicial authorities that the current government has appointed to rural districts across the republic. Just to make the job easier, Inocencio served in the Eleventh Line Battalion, the records of which can be consulted right here in Buenos Aires.

When he left Inocencio's house, Moreira spent two weeks at the house of his friend Leather Man, which, because of its isolation, constituted his last, most secure hideout.

Who was Leather Man?

xxiv

Leather Man was one of a kind. He spent all his time in the pulperías, drinking and playing cards when he had money, rarely, watching those activities when he didn't. Clothes, saddle, and bridle, everything that in Juan Moreira was first class, was third or fourth class in Leather Man. And, oh, his horse! It resembled the swaybacked old mounts they give to small-town police. His face was criss-crossed with the scars that gaucho knife fights often produce, and neither his long hair nor his black beard had ever been touched by such a thing as a comb.

Leather Man was a party animal, too—tall and skinny, with prominent cheek bones, a smile eternally on his face, and a look in his eyes that felt like someone tickling you. It just wasn't a party without Leather Man there, people said, because he was just so funny. Nobody told a joke like Leather Man.

Don't get the wrong idea, though. Leather Man carried a facón like any self-respecting gaucho. He did not pick fights, nor did he join them if given an opportunity not to, but if obliged to fight, he had the guts for it. No one had ever seen him run away or strike a treacherous blow.

Periodically, and only when he was very drunk, Leather Man went to fight the police just for sport (you see why Moreira liked him), on which occasions he typically ended up badly battered and covered with light saber wounds. The Justice of the Peace considered his advanced state of inebriation to be an extenuating circumstance and always let him go home after a few days in the stocks. He never learned his lesson for long, though.

After each episode like this, Leather Man had the habit of rubbing his wounds with cane liquor and taking his daily siesta in the full rays of the sun, a procedure that helped him heal more rapidly and without infection, as he said. And in truth, his wounds healed with remarkable speed. His nickname, Leather Man, was a tribute to this quality, a name so universally applied to him that most of his acquaintances knew no other. They joked that police sabers were rarely sharp enough to cut all the way through Leather Man's thick hide.

The storekeepers liked Leather Man because he played the guitar, made the other men laugh, bought liquor as long as he had money, and, when he didn't, happily did odd jobs around the pulpería.

Sometimes, when he wanted to fight the police, he couldn't find them, or possibly, seeing that he was so drunk he could hardly stay on his horse, the police took pity on the fool and refused to fight him. On those occasions, Leather Man returned to the pulpería saying that "all the cowards had turned tail," and he reenacted his imaginary triumph to the applause of the other men, who then bought him another drink.

"Yes, my friends," Leather Man would conclude happily, "and they talk about Juan Moreira, who isn't fit to saddle my horse!"

Such was the man of the sadly famous moniker, whom Moreira accepted and trusted as a friend, with fatal consequences.

The two met at a pulpería that had a running, high-stakes card game, much frequented by local big shots and tough guys. Leather Man had nothing to bet, so he was watching over the players' shoulders. Moreira stood at the table, deck in hand, dealing cards, taking in money or paying out, according to the cards that each player received, whether by luck or some other principle. The pile of money in front of Moreira grew and grew, and along with it, Leather Man's staring eyes, watching the glittering silver coins as if mesmerized.

Moreira had just dealt himself a high card when two boney hands were thrust in front of him, grabbing the whole pile of money, in the manner of an Assistant Justice who has spontaneously decided to prohibit gambling.

Moreira turned around quickly. If that was a joke, it wasn't funny. He struck Leather Man's face with the back of his hand.

Leather Man dropped the money and pulled his facón, and Moreira readily accepted the challenge, stepping to the middle of the room and pulling his own. Leather Man followed him with a swagger and the two squared off, face-to-face, eye-to-eye, blades at the ready. Then a change came over Leather Man, who slouched, directing his eyes at the floor and lowering his blade to the side of his leg.

"Come on, coward," said Moreira, still furious, "don't give up. This is a nice spot for a fight."

"It's no use," droned Leather Man. "You're ten times the gaucho that I am, Juan Moreira."

"Then why do you challenge the big boys, eh?" laughed Moreira, disarmed by the man's honesty and inclining not to kill him.

Leather Man scooped the money off the floor with his left hand and offered it to Moreira, simultaneously extending his right hand in a humble request for friendship. Moreira sheathed his weapon and shook Leather Man's hand somewhat disdainfully, but when the other men in the pulpería began to hoot derisively at the humiliated gaucho, he put his hand back on the heavy silver handle of his facón and asked which of them was braver than Leather Man.

Silence reigned, as the onlookers' jeers turn to ice in their mouths.

After that, Leather Man became Moreira's uninvited sidekick. Why did the famous outlaw associate with such a man? Maybe it was just to have someone amusing to converse with, because Moreira was tired of spending all his time alone. An inveterate "pulpería lizard," Leather Man became Moreira's eyes and ears in Lobos, tipping him off to the presence of Provincial Guard and Buenos Aires police anywhere in the vicinity of La Estrella, which was well known to be Moreira's favorite place to carouse. The authorities even knew which of the women who worked there was Moreira's favorite.

Outwardly, Leather Man worshiped Moreira, but inwardly he seethed with resentment and longed for revenge. He was so frightened of Moreira that he dared make no direct move against him, however, not even when the outlaw slept at his house. A change in Moreira can be deduced from the fact that he no longer slept beside his saddled horse and, to the contrary, wanted a bed. He took Leather Man's bed when at his house, and they say that the poor devil didn't close his eyes all night as Moreira snored, and yet never once thought of killing him in his sleep. He was too frightened.

Even stabbing in the back was something that Leather Man did at a distance. Each time he gave Moreira an "all clear" regarding Provincial Guard and Buenos Aires police, he let the authorities of Lobos know that the famous outlaw was heading for La Estrella to start one of his famous three-day revels.

XXV

Moreira knew that La Estrella was being watched, and still he went. He had lost the will to go on living. The thing that he cared about now was how he would die. He wanted to go down fighting, with piles of lawmen's bodies on the ground around him. On the thirtieth of April, 1874, he got his wish.

On that day, Leather Man's "all clear" was totally false. Troopers of the Buenos Aires metropolitan police and Provincial Guard had been called to augment the district police, coordinated by Eulogio Varela. The result was a small army that, for the first time in an attempt to take Moreira, combined outsiders' training and firepower with insiders' local knowledge. A number of operatives infiltrated La Estrella out of uniform.

Moreira arrived at La Estrella in the company of a tough gaucho called Julián Andrade (not his old friend Julián) whom he had invited to the party that he planned to incite there. Andrade was a worthy *compañero* who carried a pair of bronze-barreled trabucos, like the ones that had helped make Moreira's reputation.

The two men drank deeply and had lunch, each choosing a lovely woman for company, and after eating they each took a room facing the courtyard of La Estrella and entered with their companions for a romp. Crafty veterans both, they chose rooms that would allow them to put the courtyard in a crossfire, just in case.

Moreira took off his clothes and lay on the bed while his companion Laura informed him of everything that Leather Man hadn't. Something similar presumably happened in Andrade's room, and yet both men proceeded with their siestas as if totally indifferent to the army of lawmen who were, at that very moment, surrounding La Estrella. Before very long, both were sound asleep.

At two o'clock in the afternoon, with the hot, heavy air of siesta time filling the establishment, officers representing the combined anti-Moreira force entered La Estrella and talked to the owner, who denied any knowledge of the outlaw's whereabouts. The lawmen naturally proceeded to search the building, and they were wise enough to do so quietly.

One of the doors of the courtyard cubicles stood ajar for the sake of ventilation, and loud snoring could be heard within. Looking in, the lawmen saw two bronze-barreled trabucos on a chair. One lawmen lifted them quietly while several others put their guns under the sleeping man's chin. His eyes popped open, he saw that that the jig was up, and he surrendered. Capturing Juan Moreira had been almost too easy, thought these Provincial Guards, and they were right, because this was Julián Andrade, as one of the Lobos lawmen soon informed them.

Where then was Moreira?

Several lawmen gathered outside the closed door of another of the bedroom cubicles. The shrill barking of a small dog could be heard inside.

As the woman named Laura tells it, Moreira opened his eyes when he heard the Provincial Guards in the courtyard shouting that they'd found someone. Leaping up, he dressed quickly and sat on the bed loading and checking his firearms.

"Maybe they'll just take him and leave," offered Laura optimistically.

"No, they're outside the door," said Moreira, pointing his chin at Cacique, who was alternately sniffing under the door and barking furiously.

A heavy knock at the door, and Moreira waved Laura to one side of it.

"Who's there?" he inquired in a loud voice, looking at Laura, though obviously not speaking to her. She was frightened, and he sent her a comforting smile and wink.

"Open up in the name of the law," ordered the lawmen outside.

Moreira seized Laura's arm, opened the door a quarter of the way, and pushed her out of it.

Meanwhile, the small army of soldiers had taken up positions in and around the rear courtyard of La Estrella. Sharpshooters covered the door from positions across the courtyard; other police were massed on each side of door, their officers standing in front of it, talking with Moreira inside.

"Turn yourself in, Juan Moreira!"

"Turn myself in?" came the voice from inside the door. "To whom?"

"To the police of Buenos Aires," said the officer in command of those forces.

"Do you know what the Buenos Aires police can do?" asked Moreira.

And before the officers outside had considered what they might answer, if an answer were required, Moreira opened the door and stepped out. Quickly scanning the situation, he extended his arms to the left and right and fired his weapons at the soldiers massed on either side of the door, killing one soldier.

"Die!" shouted Moreira.

"Fire!" shouted their horrified officers standing in front of the door. But the officers themselves blocked the view of the sharp-shooters across the courtyard. Those on either side took a moment to recover, and Moreira ducked back inside the door before they could aim adequately. The soldiers on either side of the door found themselves pointing their weapons at each other.

The officers at the door heard Moreira thump the butts of his tra-bucos on the floor, reloading them. Then the door opened again, and this time the officers moved out of the way and the sharpshooters across the courtyard opened fire.

Moreira stepped out of the door holding his two trabucos as bullets knocked off bits of the door frame on both sides of him, and for a moment he stood still, as if to say "here I am." Then he theatrically examined himself, all still in one piece! He laughed merrily, before leveling and firing his trabucos again, one to the side and another at his admirers across the courtyard. Then, like a jack-in-the-box, he popped back inside the cubicle and closed the door.

The latest blasts had wounded the captain of the Lobos police, Eulogio Varela, in the leg.

After an interval, Moreira emerged again, holding only one trabuco, and when it didn't fire, he threw it aside, pulled his famous facón, and leapt to the center of the courtyard, where the soldiers around its perimeter would find it hard to shoot at him without hitting each other.

Varela, wounded in the leg but still standing, and Pedro Berton, the leader of the Buenos Aires police contingent, met him there sword in hand. Moreira's facón was more than a match for their two sabers, though.

Grabbing a soldier's rifle, Berton took aim at Moreira, carefully, in order not to kill one of his own men. Too carefully. Moreira drew a double-barreled pistol and shot Berton in his trigger hand, spoiling not only his aim but his ability to use the rifle at all. The young officer of Buenos Aires dropped the weapon. At that point, Moreira perfectly well could have killed Berton with a second shot, but he pushed the pistol back into his tirador.

Varela kept Moreira occupied while the wounded Berton tried to rally his discouraged men. Varela has showed me the sword that he used that day, blunted and hacked nearly through in several places by the strength of Moreira's arm and the temper of his steel blade. Varela's heroism, simply holding his own against Juan Moreira for a period of minutes, while wounded in the knee, was recognized by the watching soldiers, who were eventually shamed into joining the fight.

Now, Moreira was surrounded by soldiers attacking him with swords. The poncho wrapped around his left arm as a shield hung in tatters.

"Out of my way!" he shouted and put his hand to his waist as if going for one of his trabucos, but he no longer had either one.

Several members of the local police turned and ran, however. In their experience, that particular cry heralded death and destruction. Their out-of-town comrades chuckled as the local men sheepishly rejoined them.

"Boooo!" went Moreira, cackling with delight.

He stood now on the side of the courtyard, opposite the well, panting, his forehead matted with hair, sweat, and blood. He had been involved in mortal combat for almost half an hour, and yet his movements were as agile and powerful as ever. He seemed to have just begun to fight.

Despite the enormously unequal odds, the outcome was still not a foregone conclusion at this point, when, in another part of the building, Julián Andrade managed to break free from his bonds and ran out into the street looking for his horse. The rear wall of La Estrella's courtyard was an avenue of escape that the two outlaws had noticed upon arrival. They had left their horses on the other side of it, just in case. If Andrade could get there, he could possibly help Moreira, too.

But there was no way. The street was full of uniforms and the building, totally surrounded. Within seconds the unarmed Andrade went down with blood gushing from two saber cuts in the head, and he was soon more securely trussed up and carried back into the building where the final assault against Juan Moreira was about to begin.

As soldiers moved around the edges of the courtyard, one had advanced into it, crouching behind the well. The sadly famous Sergeant Chirino, then of the Lobos police, today a guard at the penitentiary of Buenos Aires, was about to make his immortal reputation.

Varela limped out toward Moreira and swung his sword, but the gaucho simply walked away from him.

"Go get that leg seen to, friend," said Moreira. "No more for you today."

Suddenly, Moreira noticed movement. Sharpshooters with Remington rifles were taking up positions on the roof, from which they could calmly fire down into the courtyard without fear of shooting their own men.

Deciding what to do in a split second, Moreira sprinted across the courtyard to the wall that divided it from the street where he and Andrade had left their horses. It was a rough old masonry wall, perhaps seven feet tall, with lots of protruding bricks. Putting his knife in his teeth, Moreira started climbing it.

He had both hands on the top of the wall and lacked only one or two more footholds to scramble over when he let out a bloodcurdling roar, muffled by the facón between his teeth, his right hand slipped from the top of the wall, and his right foot slipped from its foothold.

What had happened?

Moreira had run past Sergeant Chirino, crouching behind the well, without seeing him, and once Moreira was climbing the wall, Chirino had come up behind him and lanced him through the lung with the bayonet of his rifle. The bayonet went straight through Moreira's body, out his chest, and into the masonry wall to a depth of about three inches, pinning him there like an insect on an entomologist's corkboard.

Very experienced in the matter of stab wounds, Juan Moreira knew then that he had only minutes of consciousness and, probably, life. His first thought was to avenge himself against the coward who had stabbed him in the back. He spat his facón from his mouth in order to say:

"You don't stab a man like *me* in the back, little man!" and, craning around enough to see Chirino's uniform, "The 'law.' I should have known. . . ."

As he lost his footing and handhold on the right side, the weight of his body came to rest on the bayonet, which began to sag because of the softness of the bricks, although Chirino held it in place as best he could. With desperate strength, Moreira pulled his double-barreled pistol with one remaining bullet from his waist and twisted his body on the bayonet, throwing his arm behind him and down to where Chirino stood trembling with the effort to hold him up, and fired blindly but with instinctive accuracy. The bullet grazed the sergeant's left temple and lodged in his cheekbone.

Chirino toppled backward, pulling his rifle with him, and the bayonet came out of Moreira with a sickening sound and a gush of blood. Moreira slid down the wall and miraculously landed on his feet. There was his facón, and he stooped to pick it up with a bloody smile.

"I'm not dead yet, cowards!" he shouted gleefully in his classic style.

But he was moving slowly and was so close to dead that no one bothered to shoot him. Instead, everyone crowded around and pressed close to see the amazing death of Juan Moreira. A young man named Gabriel Larsen found himself mesmerized by the image of Moreira standing there, his shirt glistening with blood under his blood-matted black beard, standing more or less on the brink of hell, his eyes throwing flames at the soldiers around him.

"At me, now, come on!" shouted Moreira, amid small sprinkles of blood, beginning to stagger forward, jabbing his famous two-foot facón at the soldiers.

Larsen, in Moreira's path, failed to react, and Eulogio Varela stepped in front of him, taking in his shoulder a knife blow that otherwise would probably have killed the young man.

Moreira pulled out his knife and looked at his old friend with respect. Then he vomited blood and dropped to his knees and vomited more blood. Cacique appeared out of nowhere in front of him, and Moreira seemed to reach for him, but instead fell face down in the dirt.

The soldiers crowded close around him but jumped back when he raised his head for the last time and moved his right hand, still clutching his facón. His eyes, with the veil of death already descending, focused on the bloody head of Sergeant Chirino, who lay immobile nearby. Satisfied, Moreira lowered his head and stopped moving as the blood that remained in his body emptied from it.

xxvi

W hen the soldiers were quite sure that he was dead, they turned him over and opened his shirt. The legend existed among them that Moreira wore a coat of chainmail under his clothing, because he was not known ever to have been seriously wounded. What they found explained the mystery of Moreira's invulnerability in a different way. His chest and arms were criss-crossed with scars, nine of them, in fact, going back to his fight with Leguizamón, three of them bullet wounds. He had been very careful, it seems, always to conceal his wounds, staying hidden when wounded until he was able to move normally again.

The five men wounded in the action were cared for by surgeons whom the provincial governor provided expressly for that purpose, and a procession of curious visitors began to arrive at La Estrella to gawk at the famous corpse. The procession continued for many hours, bringing people from all the districts where he had roamed in life, people who wanted to see with their own eyes that Juan Moreira was really dead. Seeing is believing, they said.

Moreira was buried the next day in a grave marked only by a number—a number, and the presence of a little dog whom the keepers of the cemetery, a Basque woman and her husband, say lay down on the fresh earth of the new grave and slept there for several nights. The dappled bay horse, Moreira's other inseparable companion, ended up in the hands of some police sergeant or Assistant Justice, and his bronze-barreled trabucos and sliver-handled facón were remitted to the Buenos Aires criminal court, so that it could close the books forever on the most famous outlaw in nineteenth-century Argentina.

On May the fourth after siesta time, a ragged gaucho on a surprisingly fine horse rode into Lobos and asked directions to the cemetery. The people who explained the location of the cemetery were impressed by the man's hangdog expression. He failed even to thank them for their help and rode away with his chin on his chest. He must be some friend of Moreira's, they supposed, and correctly, for it was Julián. He sat by the grave for hours, and the Basque woman had to ask him twice to leave at closing time. The first time she had to tap him on the shoulder to get his attention. He took Cacique with him when he left, according to the Basque woman, who says she was surprised to see the little dog so apparently at home on the back of a horse.

Moreira's wife and son live today in Matanzas with a leading family of that locality—the Aguilar family, across from the new fire station—in a mutually beneficial arrangement that provides the two with shelter and the family with domestic service.

As for Juan Moreira, he is still alive in the collective memory of the pampas localities where he lived as an honest, hardworking gaucho and then roamed as outlaw. Go to any pulpería on the pampa today, and you'll hear men singing about Moreira. Anyone who can claim to have met him proudly tells of the experience, and many tell Moreira stories who met him only in their imaginations. All will tell you, though, about how he fought off swarms of lawmen single-handedly, and those are the stories most enjoyed in the telling.

The people of our countryside will tell you that Moreira's story is not unique at all. How many decent men have been deprived of normal, productive lives by the abuses rife among the rural Justices of our republic! What more must occur before the well-intentioned citizens of our progressive cities wake up to the iniquities that our judicial system works in the countryside?

The gaucho is a man who has, in practice, no legal rights—not even the right to a beautiful wife if the local Justice decides he wants her. We speak of a republic of laws, but for the gaucho "the law" means basically one thing: the local Assistant Justice has the right to slap you in chains, conscript you into the army, and send you to the frontier for two years, whenever he likes, and for whatever reason. It is time that gauchos enjoy the protections of the constitution that they have fought to defend in the great battles of our patriotic history.

May the rights of citizenship be enjoyed by all citizens, rich and poor, rural and urban, in every region of this land so blessed by providence, so ill-served by her public administration. That has been the great theme of this true and well-researched account of the life of Juan Moreira.

The history of the Argentine republic contains only one other outlaw whose story can rival that of Juan Moreira. I speak of Juan Cuello, who terrorized the city of Buenos Aires in the late 1840s and early 1850s.

Soon to appear, *Juan Cuello*, the new true crime novel by Eduardo Gutiérrez, is chocked with swashbuckling episodes that will delight and fascinate our readers!

Postscript

After the final installment of our story of Juan Moreira, so enthusiastically received by the reading public of Buenos Aires, and thanks to the generosity of Señor Melitón Rodríguez, I have personally examined the knife of that legendary gaucho. It is properly a museum piece, worthy to be exhibited beside the sword of El Cid, and a full description of it will certainly be of interest to all who have followed our foregoing narrative.

The weapon given him by his political patron Adolfo Alsina, the weapon with which Moreira fought his astounding battles, is quite different from the knives carried by most rural men. It is a true facón, midway in size between a large knife and a sword. From pommel to point, it measures eighty-four centimeters, sixty-three being the blade of Toledo steel. The hilt and pommel are of heavy silver, inlaid with gold, of superb workmanship, weighing together twenty-five ounces. Interestingly, the hilt that protects the hand was modified according to Moreira's instructions to make it more effective in combat.

Also following the publication of the last installment of our story, I have learned a fabulous addition to it, an anecdote that paints in authentic tints the true character of the man. This anecdote has been provided to me by Doctor Leopoldo del Campo, among the most talented and dedicated young attorneys currently practicing at the Buenos Aires bar. Among del Campo's most noble attributes is his habit of providing legal aid to poor men without access to competent legal defense.

Among the many who have benefitted from this gentleman's goodness and generosity is a poor gaucho of Navarro, Juan Almada by name. Accused of homicide, Almada was happily acquitted, but because he had only a thatched hut and few sheep and cows, he was unable to pay Almada for the brilliant defense that had established his innocence. All he could think to offer was his hospitality, there in Navarro, whenever del Campo wished to visit him.

Not many years had passed when the distinguished lawyer decided to take a vacation in the country, and how better to enjoy the simple joys of rural life than in the thatched hut of an authentic gaucho of the pampa? Talk of the famous bandit Juan Moreira did not deter him, and arriving by train in Lobos, del Campo rented a horse and set out for Navarro.

And whom should he encounter, but Juan Moreira! The man's luxurious dress, enormous facón, and two gleaming bronze-barreled trabucos permitted no mistake in the matter. Moreira greeted del Campo courteously and asked if he'd seen, on the road, a man in the company of a beautiful young woman. Del Campo replied honestly that he had, indeed, seen two such people sometime earlier, but he was unsure of the direction that they had taken.

A shadow came over Moreira's face, when he heard that news. He had an account to settle with those two. Moreira then asked what a gentleman was doing riding by himself across the pampa, and del Campo explained his visit.

Moreira knew Almada, as it happened, and when he understood that del Campo had defended Almada in court, pro bono, and established his innocence, his eyes grew big and round. The gentleman explained his idea that assuring an adequate legal defense was the only guarantee that justice would be done. For him, it was an obligation of conscience.

When Moreira understood the full measure of this gentleman's professional integrity, he felt profoundly moved and, says del Campo, he had tears in his eyes when he said good-bye, God bless, and indicated the quickest path to Almada's house.

The young gentleman, meditated for a while before continuing his journey. How could that be the "fierce bandit" Juan Moreira?

Finally, I've received the following letter and should not wish to deprive my readers of its contents:

Buenos Aires
20 March 1880

Señor don Eduardo Gutiérrez
Dear Sir:
Congratulations on the great success of your account of Juan Moreira. Here are two further anecdotes that contribute to the biography of this rare and noble personage. Both incidents occurred in the locality of San Justo, which does not figure in your account.

One year, on Friday of Holy Week, Moreira decided to shake things up by galloping around in front of the church. Because such great care had been taken to ensure a peaceful and somber mood on this holy day, five police tried to stop him. No doubt because it was Holy Week, Moreira preferred to fight the five of them with his horsewhip, employing no other weapon. Because it was warm and he wore no poncho, he defended himself by catching the soldier's saber blows with his hat in his left hand. The frustrated and humiliated soldiers finally gave up and disappeared "as fast as money in the national treasury."

On another occasion, the local police decided that it was time to capture or kill Moreira and went out to look for him. They didn't need to go far, because they found him right in town, eating lunch. Moreira got on that fast horse of his and led them on a merry chase, but when he got tired, at a place we call El Estanque, he simply stopped, unsaddled, and sat on the ground, waiting. The police kept their distance, while Moreira hooted and called them names, and they finally decided that he must have some terrible surprise prepared for them and that it would be unwise to try to capture him. So they turned around and went back to town, leaving him right there, rolling on the ground with laughter!

It is a pleasure to provide you with further grist for your mill. Your inimitable pen will no doubt fill these episodes with the vivid interest that good material always has when really well written.

Your Faithful Servant,
Julio Llanos
464 Chacabuco Street
Buenos Aires

GLOSSARY

Bota de potro: coltskin boot; the raw leather was pulled off the colt's leg and fitted directly onto a gaucho's foot with the hair on the inside, where it was left to dry; the exposed toes were a telltale sign of the bota de potro.

Caudillo: a charismatic political leader, often an adroit horseman and of military background, who provided benefits (protection, work, food) for clients and who inspired loyalty and emulation; because of these characteristics caudillos became cultural icons or heroes.

Criollo: by the second half of the 1800s this term defined what and who was "authentically" Argentine (or Uruguayan), in contrast to its colonial denomination of Spaniards born in the Americas and their privileged social status.

Facón: a long, pointed knife, often with decorative silverwork on the hilt and sheath; Gutiérrez describes Moreira's facón as "midway in size between a large knife and a sword."

Gringo: a non-native Spanish-speaking foreigner; in the late nineteenth-century Río de la Plata the term was a common reference to Italian, English, and other European immigrants, in contrast to today's more frequent association with North Americans.

Malambo: a solo dance with lightening-fast leg movements, including foot sweeps ("scrubbing" the dance floor) and boot stomping, in which men compete in a show of virtuosity, not unlike *payadores*; malambo is often danced to guitar accompaniment and always excites onlookers.

Payador: a gaucho poet and guitar player who improvised verse and who engaged with fellow roving troubadours in informal competitions called *payadas*; payadores attempted to outdo each other in improvisational skill and wit around campfires, at family and friendly gatherings, and at *pulperías,* where payadas could last hours and occasionally led to fights.

Pulpería: dry goods store that sold basic foodstuffs and that doubled as a tavern and gathering place.

Tirador: a wide leather belt worn by gauchos, often ornamented with gold and silver coins and, for those who could afford it, a fancy buckle; the tirador had pouches for carrying small items, and it served the utilitarian purpose of holding items slipped between it and its bearer's body, like a *facón* or *trabuco*.

Trabuco: short-barreled shotgun with a wide, flaring muzzle, in Moreira's case made of bronze.